FAMILY SECRETS

Angela Hood *&* Daphne Cayo

Cover and book design by PegDuVal,
PegDuVal-Art.com
Lafayette, LA, USA
Ashley Pruett, Editor
Printed in the United States of America.

1st Edition
ISBN 978-0-615-556-772

www.AngelaHood.com
Angela Hood Ministries
P.O. Box 120482
Ft. Lauderdale, FL
1-888-900-5211

Request information about the Ministry from:
PastorAngela@angelahood.com

We dedicate this book to everyone who has experienced sexual abuse and has had the courage and commitment to confront their abuser and continue to live their lives with passion and perseverance. By sharing your story, you provide hope, encouragement, and life to others who cannot because they are still living under the shadow of "the family secret."

CHAPTER 1

"The Lord is my shepherd; I shall not want."

Elizabeth stared blankly at the figures in black trying to shield themselves from the cold, pelting rain. She recognized almost everyone in attendance. As she looked around and caught people's eyes, they quickly looked away. She felt bad for making anyone else feel awkward.

Until that moment, she hadn't even realized it was raining. Now she saw that the wind and rain were blowing through the crowd of people, huddled as close together as possible to protect themselves against the elements. She looked around at the mourners as if she were a stranger looking in on someone else's funeral; floating above the scene, an alien examining the tendencies of a race of people not her own.

She didn't feel anything and hadn't since her mother's passing four days ago. Mama had gone quickly at the end. After so much pain, she had simply slipped away; her lips curved upward in a smile, her body finally relaxed in a state of eternal rest. Elizabeth had been with her mother in the final hours of her death. Even seeing the cold body in the casket earlier during the service was not enough to jerk her into reality.

'Even though I walk through the valley of the shadow of death, I will fear no evil," the tired old pastor continued. Despite the rain, he was making no attempt to shout. There was no way those in the back could hear over the pellets dropping all around them. The man directly in front of Elizabeth shivered and pulled his black trench coat up farther around his neck. *Everyone wishes he would hurry*, thought Elizabeth. For her, time seemed to be standing still.

She glanced over at her sister Ellen, who was holding her daughter Hannah near. Hannah was five years old; too young to really remember much of her grandmother. Ellen was drawing her daughter close to protect her from the weather, drawing strength from the proximity of her child. Hannah stooped down to wipe a leaf from her new shoes. They were black patent leather Mary Jane's her mother had taken her to the department store to buy yesterday. Hannah had picked them out all by herself, carried them in the fancy bag to the car, and placed them carefully at the foot of her bed to wear the next day. The dress underneath her raincoat wasn't new, but Hannah didn't care. Her shoes were so shiny and wonderful. She didn't even mind the rain on them.

Even now, Ellen could see traces of her mother in her daughter. Hannah already carried herself with a poise that seemed unnatural for a child so new to the world. Sometimes, she seemed wiser than Ellen did. She was definitely more cautious.

"Surely goodness and mercy shall follow me all the days of my life, and I shall dwell in the house of the Lord forever," Reverend Andrews finally finished. He closed his Bible and nodded an unspoken thanks to the young man behind him who was holding an umbrella over the book. Gingerly, he tucked the Bible into his breast pocket and closed his eyes for a few moments in respect for the dead.

The group of mourners uttered a collective, "Amen," as Reverend Andrews finished. A few in the back ushered their small children back towards their cars. The Reverend nodded to Elizabeth and Ellen, and they slowly approached the side of the freshly dug grave, each grasping a single pink rose.

To look at them, you wouldn't know they were sisters. Ellen's figure was poised beautifully against the dull grey backdrop of the sky. Elegantly dressed in a tailored black shift dress and belted overcoat, she pulled her blonde hair back into a neat bun at the nape of her slender neck. Even in this stressful time, in the midst of terrible weather, not a hair was out of place and her make-up and nails were miraculously impeccable. There was nothing about her appearance that would signal grieving; rather, she seemed completely in control. She had chosen a single strand of pearls around her neck and paired them with her mother's understated pearl earrings. Although one could clearly see the pain and loss in her eyes, she maintained her usual level of composure and allowed only a single tear to trace down her cheek, blending with the rain.

Elizabeth was nothing like Ellen in looks or personality. Her dress, bought at the local thrift store, hung loosely over her slim body. It was quite possible one would notice her clothing more than the girl who was wearing the oversized outfit. Her chestnut hair was wet and plastered against her face, which she hadn't bothered to fix with make-up. Her ragged, bitten nails ruined the grace of her long fingers.

As Reverend Andrews finished the eulogy, she couldn't stop the tears from coursing down her face, making no effort to control the sobs racking through her body. As poised and precise as Ellen appeared, Elizabeth seemed sloppy and unkempt. To one, the mourners felt sadness, to the other, pity. While Ellen was conscious of how those in attendance glanced at Elizabeth, Elizabeth herself seemed completely unaware her cries were making others uncomfortable.

Hannah, a miniature version of her mother, shifted her gaze from one woman to the other, waiting for a sign telling her what to do. With her curly golden locks and large blue eyes, she looked like an angel guarding over her grandmother's grave. Ellen gently guided her forward and threw her rose into the grave. She nodded to Hannah to do the same, only to watch her little girl hesitate, unwilling to let the beautiful flower go. Ellen leaned down beside her daughter and whispered into her ear as she brushed a crease out of the girl's dress and tightened her hair bow. Slowly, Hannah released the rose and the two of them watched as it drifted down into the dark hole. Hannah leaned over the grave, trying hard to find her rose in the pile of dirt.

"Come on, baby," Ellen whispered, grabbing her daughter's hand. Hannah smiled up at her Aunt Elizabeth as she, too, staggered toward the open pit. Hannah glanced down at her shoes and noticed some of the dirt from the open grave was stuck to the heel of the left. Without thinking, she bent down and used the back of her coat to wipe away the mud. *There*, she thought to herself, *all nice and shiny*.

The scent of wet earth so overpowered Elizabeth, she stood frozen in place. At that moment, all the emotions from the past few weeks washed over her, the smell of earth filling her nostrils and making her stomach turn. She   *3* started to double over, wishing more than anything she was back alone in the house with her mother.

Maybe if I don't move, I'll wake up from this nightmare, she said to herself. This time, she was acutely aware of dozens of eyes upon her, waiting for her. Her breath came in short, rapid bursts, threatening to cause her to faint. "How am I going to survive without you, Mama?" She whispered so softly into the sheet of rain no one else heard. Her dad had walked away from their family when she was only seven years old. She thought it was her fault, and no matter how hard her mother tried to convince her otherwise, she still felt the same way. She wondered if her life would be any different if her dad had stayed.

"My goodness, snap out of it, will you, Liz?" Ellen hissed in her ear. She grabbed Elizabeth by the elbow and gently but firmly propelled her toward the open grave. Elizabeth closed her eyes and looked away as she let go of the pink rose, unable to watch its descent. She was vaguely aware of Ellen guiding her towards the car that was to take them back to their home; a home that would forever mark itself with the absence of her mother's presence. A home Elizabeth couldn't help but think would never feel like home again.

She could see Hannah walking in front of them, stepping carefully around muddy puddles so as not to soil her patent leather shoes and pristine white tights. Even though the little girl tried to stay clean, she was unknowingly splattering mud up the back of her tights. Elizabeth could hear the muted whispers of the other mourners also heading back to their vehicles, already discussing the weather and what they should have for dinner. She felt like she was walking through a dense fog. Everything seemed so far away and surreal.

When they approached the car, it took all of her concentration just to step inside the vehicle. She caught a glimpse of Ellen, who had already climbed into the driver's seat and fastened her seat belt and was now looking impatiently at Elizabeth. She pulled herself together, but inside, she desperately wanted to run to the grave and fling herself inside to snuggle against the cold, wooden casket. She glanced behind her and saw that the graveyard workers were already filling the hole with the loose earth. The weight of the wet earth seemed heavy, and their brows furrowed in concentration while their parkas failed to keep them from getting soaked by the rain.

"Ashes to ashes…" she whispered, wiping the tears from her face with the back of her hand.

"What?" Ellen asked. "For goodness sake, at least use a tissue, Elizabeth," Ellen said and threw a wad into the backseat. Ellen lowered the visor and retouched her makeup in the car mirror.

Elizabeth slid into the car, gathering her coat around her and hugging it tightly. She stared out the window as the car pulled away from the cemetery, watching people with umbrellas hurry down the street while a young couple kissed in a doorway, hoping to outlast the rain; while other people were going about their lives… Elizabeth had no idea where her life was headed. She was unsure on how she would get there, or even if she still wanted to go. Hannah slid her delicate hand into her aunt's and squeezed tightly. The little girl crossed her legs and looked up at her aunt with her big, doe-like eyes. "You want some candy, Aunt Liz?" She asked, pulling out a pack of lemon sours from her pocket.

Elizabeth glanced down at the little, wet poof beside her on the seat… her darling Hannah. As hard as her mother was, Hannah was soft and gentle, just like her grandmother.

"Grandma would have said you looked pretty today, Hannah," Elizabeth said. "She would have been so proud of you." Elizabeth choked back tears, thinking again of her niece releasing a rose into her grandmother's grave.

Hannah stared up at Elizabeth with her beautiful, wide eyes, completely void of the day's pain. "Are we going to see Grandma again?" she asked.

Ellen peered through the rear-view mirror, "We've already talked about that, Hannah," she said, "Remember? Grandma is gone. She's with Jesus now. She's safe and she's not sick anymore, baby."

Hannah's smiled widened. "Is she with the angels, Aunt Elizabeth?" she asked as she pulled a Kleenex out of her child-sized purse and wiped her aunt's face. "It's okay. I don't think angels cry." She popped a lemon sour into her mouth.

Elizabeth drew some comfort and strength from this pure, simple gesture. She could hear Ellen talking from the front seat but made no effort to listen. She closed her eyes, resting her head against the back of the seat.

Angela Hood & Daphne Cayo

CHAPTER 2

The Carter house was a two-and-a-half-story red brick Victorian on 72nd Place in the South Shore area of Hyde Park in Chicago. Cars lined both sides of the street as friends and family, all of the mourners, gathered for the brief reception. By the time, Ellen pulled into the garage in the back of her mother's house; church members had already opened the doors and were ushering people in from the cold and rain.

Elizabeth followed Ellen, mimicking her, every move as she took off her coat, hung it up in the hall closet, and stood next to her sister in the front hallway of their childhood home; accepting comforting words and hugs as the last of the visitors entered. There was quite a spread on the table, and the smell of potato salad, fried chicken, and baked beans wafted from the kitchen and spread throughout the house.

Elizabeth looked around, trying to find an empty space to just sit and relax for a few moments. She tried to steal away to her bedroom, but everywhere she looked, friends and family were blocking her way, leaning against walls and sitting on the floor. Her feet were cold as she walked through the house. She had instinctively taken off her shoes when she entered the back door, and her nylons were wet from the rain dripping off the visitors. She felt clammy and chilled, her headache slowly intensifying the longer everyone stayed.

Ellen was the dutiful one, mingling and chatting, working the crowd of people with ease. She glanced at her sister, out of the corner of her eye, and watched as Elizabeth slipped silently through the double French doors into the dining room. Most people had already visited the spread of sandwiches and finger foods, waiting in anticipation for the hot foods to come out from the church women in the kitchen. Old women were sitting around the table, their shoulders hunched over steaming hot cups of tea and coffee, chatting in between bites of whatever was on their plates.

Elizabeth felt useless and found herself absentmindedly sweeping crumbs off the white tablecloth and straightening the dark green runner. The creamer needed a refill and she picked up the little porcelain cow grateful for a job to do, no matter how menial it seemed. She carried it to the large, bright kitchen and walked towards the refrigerator to refill it. She opened the refrigerator door and stared at its contents blankly. The usually well-stocked fridge was barren except for a gallon of soured milk and a few condiments the church women brought for the feast. She stared at the shelves, trying to remember what brought her there in the first place. She shook her head and muttered, "The creamer," as she reached in for the half-and-half and filled up the little cow. She instinctively turned toward the stove, expecting to see her mother standing at the oven, putting "all her love," as she would say, into whatever she was cooking. Instead of her mother, she saw several women she didn't recognize heating up various dishes on the old gas burners.

After filling the creamer, Elizabeth stood and looked out the window behind the sink. She gazed at the well-shaded yard and the old tire swing hanging from a branch of the ancient oak tree. She used to sit in that swing for hours, swaying back and forth in rhythm with her thoughts. Ellen always had many friends and, invariably, one or two of them would be at the house every day. Ellen didn't like having Elizabeth around when her friends were there and would go to great lengths to make sure she and her friends weren't bothered. Since Elizabeth didn't really have any friends of her own, she would, more often than not, find solace in the sounds and smells of their backyard.

Elizabeth had been the black sheep of the family, not necessarily in attitude but in looks and demeanor. Ellen had inherited their mother's golden good looks and charming personality. While Rose, her mother, used her personality to volunteer and help, Ellen mainly used hers to advance her own agenda. Elizabeth would often trail behind her mother, delivering food to the sick or offering help to the elderly in their town; silently busying herself, hoping the conversation never turned to her. Mother had been so active in the community until she got sick a few years ago.

Ellen had the same big, blue eyes, framed by long, full lashes and perfectly arched brows. Her nose was thin and delicate and turned up ever so slightly at the tip. Her mouth had been a perfect rosebud as a child and had grown into the type of pout men dreamed of. Her skin was like alabaster but always had a healthy glow. Ellen was thin but curvy in all the right places. Her posture was impeccable and she moved with a quiet grace and confidence. Everyone noticed her when she walked into a room, flashing her dazzlingly white smile.

Elizabeth had the same fair skin as Ellen, but it was framed with straight, brown hair instead of honey curls. She seldom wore her hair down, opting instead for a simple ponytail. Her eyes were almond shaped and a beautiful, rich brown with gold flecks, but people seldom noticed since she was always seemed to be looking down. Elizabeth was even slimmer than her sister, almost too thin. Even though her arms and legs were long and graceful, she lacked the curves that always drew men to Ellen. Her figure was closer to that of an adolescent schoolgirl than of a young woman ready to take on the world. She could be graceful and beautiful if she wanted, but instead tended to hunch over and shuffle her feet to avoid being noticed. It usually worked, and people quickly forgot she was in the room.

Elizabeth hurried from the kitchen when a group of women entered, shuffling past them unnoticed. Unlike her mother, Elizabeth was painfully shy. She saw Ellen at the far end of the living room, chatting away gracefully with some church women. Unlike Elizabeth, Ellen always managed to be friends with everyone. Ellen had always been the pretty one and Elizabeth the smart one. Instead of playing with friends or flirting with boys, Elizabeth tucked herself in her room and buried her nose in a book. In spite of this, it was Ellen who had the successful career while Elizabeth was unemployed. Ellen managed to earn her nursing degree from Chicago State University, while raising her daughter Hannah. Being a single mom, she'd gotten a job at Mercy Hospital soon after Hannah was born. Elizabeth was halfway towards completing her degree in biological sciences at the University of Chicago when her mother was diagnosed with ovarian cancer. Since they couldn't afford a nurse and Ellen needed to work to provide for Hannah, Elizabeth reduced her class load to take care of their mother. By the end of the year, Elizabeth's grades suffered and her mother was requiring even more care. She realized she would have to put her degree on hold and care for their mother full time while the disease slowly spread through her body.

Now, as she stood in her childhood home, staring out the kitchen window, she wondered what she was to do with herself now. Her mother's treatments, medications and other medical needs completely exhausted what little savings they had accumulated over the years. Her mother re-mortgaged the house, sold the car, and cashed in every asset she could think of to pay her growing medical debt. It had not been enough, and Elizabeth had five weeks to move out of her childhood home before the bank took possession. Any money from the sale of the home above what was owed to the bank was already earmarked for paying the remaining medical bills. Elizabeth had no home, no money, no education, and no job. She was losing almost everything that ever mattered to her and felt more alone than she ever had in her life.

Looking around, Elizabeth noticed the crowd had begun to thin out as more and more people headed back into the rain, trying to get home before the sunset and visibility became poor. The few stragglers that were left were those who'd come to help with the food.

"Lizzie, dear," spoke a voice. Elizabeth turned and saw Myra Davis, a hunched over old woman with a penchant for gossip. She had the look of age and wisdom and was well respected, or perhaps feared, within the church.

"Ms. Davis," said Elizabeth, straightening up, "thank you so much for coming and helping."

Myra smiled. "I made the blackberry pies," she said, frowning when Elizabeth didn't say anything. "Don't tell me you didn't have any! I thought they were your favorite." Elizabeth grimaced. Myra Davis had a way of telling you your likes and dislikes; pegging you for affinities, you didn't know you had.

"What are your plans now, dear?" she asked. Elizabeth was taken aback by the question and looked down.

"I haven't really thought about it yet," she said. "I've been so busy taking care of Mother that I just…—"

Myra interrupted her. "Nonsense," she said. "Rose would have wanted you to move on. I have a nephew about your age that I'll send over for you to meet." Elizabeth opened her mouth in protest but Myra lifted a hand. "No need to thank me, Lizzie. I'm just here to help and do what Rose would want me to do. See you later, then," she said, patting Elizabeth on the cheek as she passed. Elizabeth watched as she walked past Ellen and patted Hannah on the head. Whatever she said to Ellen, Elizabeth knew it did not sit well, either, as she saw her sister's body tense with the conversation.

As Myra walked out the front door, Ellen turned towards Elizabeth and rolled her eyes. "That woman," she said. "I don't know why Mother ever bothered with her." Ellen looked around at the house. Although the church ladies had cleaned up as well as they could, there were still a few scattered paper plates and plastic cups splashed throughout the house. Mud droplets lay dry and crusted on the carpet; the rugs by the front and back doors soaked.

Angela Hood & Daphne Cayo

CHAPTER 3

The last of the guests had finally headed out, braving the wind and rain. Ellen had put Hannah down for a nap in her old bedroom and the two sisters were now sitting quietly in the kitchen, not knowing what to say to each other. Ellen finally broke the silence that seemed to reverberate off the walls.

"Where were you all afternoon?" she asked in a tone typically reserved for her most annoying patients. "You left me to deal with all the pats on the arm, sympathetic looks, and crocodile tears."

"I only went to the kitchen for a few minutes to fill the creamer. Old Mrs. Adams from the women's group at the church cornered me. She was telling me about the time Mom swatted Reverend Bennett's hand when he tried to swipe one of her famous date squares at the church bazaar."

"God! How many times have we heard that story? I swear, one of the old bags in the women's group told that story every time she was at the house. You know, I don't think they ever actually did anything at those meetings other than complain about their husbands or other people's children while sipping tea and scarfing down cookies. Myra was the worst."

The sisters worked in silence, one carrying dishes to the kitchen as the other washed them. It wasn't until everything had been cleared that Ellen and Elizabeth sat down, each lost in her own thoughts.

"The house seems so big and empty without Mom in it. I mean, I know she was a small woman and all, but her presence really filled the room," Elizabeth sighed.

"I know what you mean. You could always smell her perfume mixed with whatever she was baking that day. You could hear her talking to herself as she pulled gum wrappers and hair clips out of our pockets when she did the laundry."

"I can still hear her singing her favorite hymns off key in the shower."

"Want something to drink?" Ellen asked as she stood and walked to the ancient fridge. "We've got cranberry juice, milk, and water, or I could put the kettle on if you would like some tea."

"Tea is okay if you don't mind. My clothes still feel damp from the rain, and I can't seem to get warm."

Ellen put the kettle on the front burner of the stove and turned on the gas burner underneath. Elizabeth had bought her mother a new electric kettle for Christmas when she was sixteen. She had gotten a part-time job that year shelving books at the library. Her mother had thanked her and told her how much she loved the gift. But after just one week of using the kettle, it had been placed in the back of a cupboard and the whistling kettle found its way back onto the stovetop. Their mother was an old-fashioned creature of habit. She still had a rotary phone, her television was the kind with knobs on the front to turn it on and off, and she loved the sound the kettle made when it was ready for a good pot of tea.

Ellen excused herself to go and check on Hannah while they waited for the kettles high-pitched wail. Elizabeth busied herself making a tray of sandwiches and goodies for them to eat with their tea. She wasn't very hungry, but she knew she hadn't eaten in over a day and should at least try to swallow a few bites of sandwich. She was setting the plate on the table just as the kettle whistled and Ellen entered the room.

"She's sleeping like a baby. I didn't think she would go to sleep without Cindy."

Cindy was Hannah's favorite doll. Elizabeth had given it to Hannah on her third birthday. The doll actually looked quite a bit like Hannah until numerous trips down the slide at the park, daily tea parties and hours spent in the sandbox turned Cindy into a shadow of her former self. Ellen had to pry the doll from Hannah's arms while she was sleeping just to throw her in the wash. It had reached the point, however, where not even the washing machine could help poor Cindy.

Sitting at the table, as they drank their tea and stared at the sandwiches, Ellen finally asked the question they had both been avoiding.

"Have you made any arrangements yet for when the bank… you know?"

"No. I thought about going to the library this week and seeing if they had any jobs available, but it doesn't even pay enough for an apartment. I don't have a degree and I have no experience in any other areas."

"I guess you could move in with Hannah and me until you save up enough for a down payment on an apartment. You would have to get a job, though, and help out around the house. I would also expect you to contribute a little each month for groceries and expenses and stuff. I only have two bedrooms, so you can either bunk with Hannah or you could take the couch."

Elizabeth was grateful for the offer but wished there was another solution. She knew she would be going from looking after their mother to looking after Hannah. She loved Hannah and certainly didn't mind spending time with her, but she was very aware she would end up babysitting while Ellen worked and went on her many dates.

"Thanks. That would be really helpful," Elizabeth managed to say with what she hoped looked like a genuine smile.

"Well, I guess that settles it. We'll need to go through everything here at the house and figure out what we are going to do with it. I don't have a lot of room for furniture and stuff, so we could either sell it or put it in storage somewhere for when you get a place of your own. We can figure that out later. Right now I just want to get some sleep."

"Me too," said Elizabeth, although she knew she would not get any more sleep tonight than she had gotten in the last four days. Every time she closed her eyes, memories would flash on the black screen that was the back of her eyelids. She was tired of closing her eyes only to open them again when tears began to fall. She wondered if she would ever get a good night's sleep again.

Ellen excused herself and headed up to bed. Elizabeth listened for the pattern of creaks on the stairs, something that had become so familiar to her over the years. In the end, when her mother was confined to her room, *15*

Elizabeth missed the sounds of the stairs creaking, alerting her to her mother's presence.

Glancing around the front room, everything Elizabeth rested her eyes on reminded her of her mother. The room bore her fragrance, her touch, and the emptiness and loneliness of it all made Elizabeth shudder. Her mother's presence was so big in life it wasn't going away that easily in death, but it was only the remnants of a woman now gone forever.

She walked over and sat down in her mother's favorite chair; the armchair in front of the big picture window that gave her a perfect view of the neighborhood and old Mrs. Hench across the street. She used to sit and laugh with her mother at the old woman's ridiculous straw hats and nylons pulled up to just below her knees, as she worked in her front garden on summer days. Their street had been full of life when they were growing up, but now it was mostly aging men and women; the life coming back every now and then when grandchildren would visit.

She turned her cheek and smelled the fabric, her mother's presence surrounding her as she sat in the chair. She looked down and saw the last novel her mother had been reading before the pain got too bad to focus on something as simple as words on a page. *I should have read to her more,* she thought, a wave of guilt flooding over her. Instinctively, she reached down into the crack between the cushion and the chair and pulled out her mother's reading glasses. Closing her eyes, she could see her mother pushing a book closed, removing her glasses, and sticking them in the crack. She imagined her mother wiping her tired eyes after the strain of reading the fine print.

"It's been a long day," she heard Rose saying. "Why don't you get some rest?"

"I can't, Mama," Elizabeth said into the darkness, her eyes still clamped shut. "I can't sleep without you in the next room, snoring away like you do."

"Sure you can, sugar," her mother said. "You've got to. Life goes on, honey, whether you want it to or not."

"I don't want it to," Elizabeth whispered. "I feel like I was buried out there with you." Elizabeth knew the insanity of talking to her mother in the blanket of darkness, but she felt closer to her in this moment than she had since her mom died. Her eyes still closed, she could almost feel her mother drawing closer to her, laying her hand over hers, both of them resting on the armchair.

"You've got to," her mother said. "I didn't raise my girl to sit around and mope. You've got a whole life to live."

The tears were flowing down Elizabeth's cheeks, but she dared not move her hand and brush them away. She wanted this moment to last forever, and she knew if she opened her eyes or wiped away her tears she would be ushered back into the harsh reality of sleeplessness and heartache; faced with the fact that it was her own craziness, not reality, that felt her mother's presence. "I love you, Mama," she said.

"I love you too, Liz," she heard her mother's voice say. "Now get on up to bed." At this, Elizabeth opened her eyes and looked around. For a split second, she'd convinced herself when she opened her eyes her mother would be standing in front of her. Instead, she was met with the coldness of the night. The rain had started pounding again on the pavement and tapping off the window. She thought of the muddy mess it was making of her mother's grave and of how much Rose would have enjoyed it. Her mother always loved a good thunderstorm. "After rain comes life," she would say to Elizabeth.

CHAPTER 4

Everything in the house looked foreign to Elizabeth; all pockmarked with the yard sale labels. Nothing seemed priced right, so little money for so many memories. She watched as Ellen carried box after box out to the front yard, carelessly dropping items along the way. Elizabeth bent down to pick up an old, beat-up photo frame and couldn't help but smile. Mother didn't throw anything away.

"Geez, Elizabeth, can you help out a little bit?" Ellen snapped. "I'm breaking my back trying to get things ready, and you're just standing there."

Elizabeth tossed the frame into the nearest box and hefted it onto her lift hip. "Sorry, Ellen. It's just that I feel like we're selling a piece of me, you know? You moved out a while ago, but I never left. And while I'm grateful for moving in with you and Hannah, it's still not really my home, you know? This is."

Ellen sighed and shifted her weight uncomfortably. "Look, Elizabeth, about that…" She reached out and took the box from Elizabeth's arms, placing it back on the floor. "I know what I said, that you could move in and all, but that's not going to work anymore."

Elizabeth stared at the ground. "What's his name?" she asked coldly.

"It's not like that," Ellen said. "I mean, it is a guy, but he's different. He's in it for the long haul, and he absolutely adores Hannah as if she were his own." Ellen rubbed her forehead and sighed again. "I can't take care of you forever, Elizabeth. You've got to make your own way in the world. Mother's dead."

"You don't think I know that?" Elizabeth said hotly. "You know I don't have anywhere to go. I've been putting in resumes but nothing has turned up yet. What am I supposed to do, Ellen? Tell me! What am I supposed to do?"

Elizabeth knew she had gone too far. Ellen's face turned red and she spewed back, "You are not my problem, Elizabeth! Sell all of this crap, take the money, and get on with your life!" She stormed out the front door. Elizabeth could hear her slamming items onto card tables and flinging merchandise across the yard.

"Well, I guess that's it," she said to no one in particular. "I guess that's it."

"I guess that's it, Ms. Carter," the bank manager smiled, "and Ms. Carter," he said as he nodded at Ellen. "As you can see, there's simply nothing we can do. Your mother was behind on the mortgage, and…" He paused and looked at Ellen, grabbing her hand to stroke it and wink. Elizabeth watched as her sister snatched her hand back. "While we are so sorry for your loss, there's simply nothing we can do. You have a month, Ms. Carter, to get your things out before the bank repossesses. Of course, sometimes we can be persuaded to put it off if situations are desperate." He looked at Ellen again, only this time his gaze was more intense. He reminded Elizabeth of a dog in heat.

Ellen stared at Elizabeth, waiting for her to say something, anything. She had been completely silent since they entered the bank, watching in a voiceless fog as the manager talked through the situation. "Well, thank you anyway, Mr. Bosch. We'll…" she glanced at her sister. "I'll make sure everything is out and gone by then. I can assure you, there will be no need for persuasion of any kind," she said as she stood up and cinched her coat tighter around her waist. "Is there anything else we need to do today?"

"No, not today," he said, closing the file folder and placing it back in his desk drawer. Ellen walked out of the office and Elizabeth followed.

"That's that," Elizabeth said to Ellen when they got in the car.

"That jerk," Ellen replied. "*Sometimes we can be persuaded…* I should call and report him to the national office." She took a swig of the cola sitting in the cup dispenser. "Let's just go home. I have to pick up Hannah from ballet practice, anyway."

The rest of the day was spent in silence as customers came and went from the yard sale. Elizabeth was in agony, watching her mother's precious memories go for so little, but Ellen seemed to be on cloud nine, haggling their mother's life away to the highest bidder, even down to her nightshirts and church hats. By the end of the day, there were only a few tables left; the final scattered pieces of junk no one wanted.

"It's enough for at least a few months' rent," Ellen said to Elizabeth. "I won't take any of it. You can have it all." She pushed the money into Elizabeth's hand. "Consider it a fresh start, you know?"

Elizabeth stared at the money. "Yeah, a fresh start. That's just what I need," she said sarcastically.

"Goodness, Elizabeth, I really don't get you sometimes," Ellen, said. "What do you want from me?" She looked at Elizabeth, waiting for her to answer. After a few seconds of silence, she tossed her hands up, rolling her eyes. "I give up! The church charity center will be here in the morning to get the leftovers. You can clean up. I have to get home to Hannah before Jack leaves for work."

"So that's his name? Jack?"

Ellen had opened her mouth to speak when her eye caught something on the table. It was her mother's old teapot. Memories flooded over her of late nights up with her mom, pouring out heartaches and dreaming big dreams over a cup of freshly steamed tea. She remembered one night in particular when she had come home late, missing curfew, from a date that hadn't ended well. Her mascara had run all over her face by the time she walked in the house.

"You're late," Mama had said sternly, but as soon as she saw Ellen, her entire demeanor softened. "And you look cold. Come on, darling; let's have a cup of tea." Like so many other relationships, that one had ended heavy and bad. Ellen could still remember her mother's advice. "Too many men see women as welcome mats. They'll step on you because you invited them in, use you, and then move on. You're not a welcome mat, honey; you're a jewel. And nobody wipes mud on a jewel!"

Ellen smiled at the memory of her mother. She looked up and tried to catch her sister's eyes. "You know, I wish it were different. I wish we still had Mother too," she said as her fingers rested on the handle. "Goodbye, Elizabeth." She walked away before her sister saw the tears in her eyes.

CHAPTER 5

The cold brick tenement loomed large before her. It seemed there wasn't a single brick that made it through the latest graffiti war unscathed. The building was scattered with profane words and gang symbols. It was the kind of building she would usually walk by a little bit faster, clutching her purse to her chest for added security — not the type of place where you would willingly unload your possessions.

She closed her eyes and tried to remember the double French doors, pastel blue paint and Victorian lampshades of her mother's home. That life seemed so far away now. It had only been a few months since she threw her pink rose in the grave of her mother and watched the dirt being piled carelessly on top. The numbness wouldn't go away, no matter how hard she tried to focus on what needed to be done. She almost wished she'd died with her mother. She wasn't sure which was harder: losing her mother or being left to face a lifetime without her.

"Are you Elizabeth Moore?" Elizabeth snapped her head around and saw an old man who couldn't have been more than five feet tall even if his back weren't humped over. "Elizabeth Moore?" he said again. "My new tenant for 5A?"

Elizabeth composed herself. "Um, yes, that's me. I'm the one who called about the vacant apartment." She felt like a child, play-acting, moving away from home. She half expected him to ask her if her mother was waiting in the car.

"My name's Gary, Gary Jones," he said and led her inside, past a busted hallway light and into a dimly lit, musty, one-bedroom apartment. She gasped as a cockroach crawled from the living room into the kitchen and underneath the stove. She looked at Gary to see his reaction, but he stood unmoved. "Well? You takin' it?" he asked abruptly.

"I…" Elizabeth looked around and clutched the money from the yard sale in her purse. "I'll take it," she finally forced herself to say. "Here's the first month's rent." She handed over the money before she had the courage to pass on the deal. The truth was there was no other deal. This was it. The bank had come early this morning to repossess the house. Elizabeth must have looked alone and frightened because the bank officer had offered to pay for a cab to take her somewhere.

Gary counted the wad of bills three times before he handed over the keys and issued a receipt. "Rent's due on the first of every month, no grace period," he said. He turned to leave and then looked back at her, his eyebrows furrowed. "You're young and pretty," he said. "I would watch yourself around here. That can be a bad combination." Elizabeth nodded and latched the door behind him.

She unloaded the final two suitcases, all she had left of her former life; a few clothes and some miscellaneous items she couldn't part with. Whoever lived in the apartment before her left an old, 1960's-style kitchenette table, and chairs. The linoleum seat cushion covers were both slashed through. She heard footsteps and shouting in the hall and hastily pushed the table in front of the door. Leaning back against the wall, she couldn't keep her composure any longer. Her small frame slid down the wall, cracked, dry paint chips sticking to her sweater as her body fell, crumpling on the coffee stained carpet. The tears came in swells, overcoming her and racking her small frame.

"Oh, God," she said in between sobs, "I miss her so much." She gathered her skirt around her as another cockroach scurried across the floor, centimeters away from her left foot. She jerked her foot back and let out a stifled shriek. From the view, she noticed the scum on the linoleum; years of lazy house cleaning had taken its toll on the apartment. This actually cheered her up a little bit, thinking of all the cleaning the place required. At least it's something to do, she thought to herself.

Pulling herself up off the floor, she began tussling around in her belongings. At first, she was trying to keep things neat, but then, when she could not find it, she started to panic, throwing items across the room. Before she knew it, her clothes, undergarments, and papers were flung around the apartment.

Finally, she stopped and looked down. There it was, buried at the bottom of the bag. She remembered now how she wrapped it in her winter coat to make sure it didn't break. It was an old picture of her mother; a black and white photograph from her college days. It was almost like looking at a mirror image of Ellen's face. Her mother wasn't alone in the picture; there was a tall, incredibly handsome, and mysterious looking man beside her. He had his arm slung lazily across her shoulders and was looking off in the distance with a cigarette hanging out the left of his mouth. That man was her father, the mysterious man whom she had never met. She remembered the day she saw the picture in the trash can.

"Mama, who is that man," she'd asked innocently.

Mama wiped her forehead and looked down at her youngest daughter. "Your daddy, honey. That's the man who helped bring my little jewel into this world. Just 'cause he ain't here doesn't mean you ain't special," she was quick to say. She leaned down to her daughter's eye level. "Your daddy leaving had nothing to do with who you are inside," she said and lightly tapped her daughter's chest.

Elizabeth remembered asking her mother for the picture. "Can I have it?" she had said. She remembered the moment because her mother started crying and looked away from her daughter. She must have nodded her head because the picture remained in Elizabeth's care from then on.

She gently stroked the lint from her coat off the glass and set the picture on the table.

Next, she walked into the bedroom and over to the closet. Someone had tied a neon pink string of yarn onto the switch. The original chain had long since broken off. She pulled the string and a soft glow filled the room. As in the kitchen, the paint here was chipping away on every inch of the wall, but some past resident had hand-painted beautiful daisies to make a border. She couldn't help but think about the irony of someone taking such good care of such a crummy apartment. The paint was faded and someone had methodically chipped away at just about every petal, but you could at least tell what the artist had intended. Elizabeth closed her eyes and imagined herself standing in a field full of daisies. She imagined her father and mother standing in the middle of the field, holding hands and lovingly waiting for her to catch up. She opened her eyes, half expecting herself to be out of the apartment.

Elizabeth tossed her sleeping bag onto the floor and piled her suitcases into a corner. Opening the duffel bag, she pulled out her mother's old teapot, snatched away from the Goodwill pile at the last minute. Turning on the kitchen faucet, she waited until the brown water turned clear and filled up the pot. She placed a single bag of Chamomile tea into the pot and turned the stove on, waiting patiently for the gentle hiss. This was slowly starting to feel like home.

CHAPTER 6

"You know, people often say that when God closes one door, another one opens," Reverend Andrews began, "and today is testament to that fact. When your mama passed away almost six months ago, we were all grieving, Ellen. We wondered what would become of her children, of her grand-daughter. If you had told me we'd be celebrating your marriage today, I wouldn't have believed it. I love you, sweetie, and your mama is smiling down today." The Reverend gathered his composure before he turned to face the wedding guests. "Ladies and gentlemen, I now present to you, Mr. and Mrs. Jack Edwards!" The applause erupted as Jack grabbed Ellen's arm, scooped up Hannah in his arms, and walked down the aisle.

Elizabeth followed suit, her tea length lavender dress flowing behind her. She reached for her sister's hand in the vestibule. "I'm so happy for you, Ellen," she said as she bear hugged her older sister. "I really am," she repeated, pulling away to look her sister in the eye.

Ellen couldn't stop the tears and this time didn't even try. "I'm so happy, Elizabeth! I know things haven't gone as you'd like, but thanks for being here with me. I needed you up there, you know?" The two embraced once again, and then Elizabeth stepped out of the way, as the receiving line began.

Three months prior, when Ellen first told Elizabeth she was engaged, things had not been so warm and fuzzy. The couple hadn't even been dating six months, and the whole thing felt rushed and heated. "Why the hurry?" Elizabeth questioned. "You barely even know him, Ellen!"

"I know enough," Ellen had retorted. "Elizabeth," Ellen said sharply, "can't you allow me one happiness?" Can't you just be happy for me that I finally found someone who's not a bum? Jack has a real job, a future, and he loves *27*

Hannah. I'm not young anymore, Elizabeth. I've made my mistakes, and guys like Jack don't come along for girls like me."

Elizabeth had rushed to her sister's side and grabbed her hand. "Don't settle, Ellen, don't. Remember what Mama always said? You are a jewel. You and Hannah deserve the best."

Ellen had jerked her hand away and picked up her purse from the chair. "I'll have to sanitize this when I get home," she said after glancing around the apartment. "I'm not settling, Elizabeth, and, honestly, you are in no place to give anyone relationship advice, or any kind of life advice for that matter. Just be happy for me and let it be. Focus on yourself. Focus on getting out of this dump."

"Ellen, I didn't mean to make you upset. I just… "

"You just what, Elizabeth? You and Mama are just the same. She was always telling me I was going after the wrong guys; warning me to stay away from men and not make the same mistakes she did. I'm sick of all that! This is our reality, Elizabeth! Girls like us don't have the fairy tale version of life. Mama was sick in the head about that, all that talk about us being special and God giving us more in life. Mama left us, Elizabeth. She is gone. I'm marrying Jack and we're going to be happy." She started walking towards the door.

Elizabeth was crying. "Ellen, you don't know what you're saying. You are just upset. You don't mean that about Mama. She loved you. She loved me."

Ellen turned around, her petite frame halfway into the hallway. "Mama not loving you was never the problem," she said and slammed the door.

Elizabeth and her sister didn't speak for two and a half months. Ellen planned the wedding without her, and it was only when she received the invitation in the mail a week before had she even known she was invited. When Ellen showed up at her apartment with the bridesmaid's dress, Elizabeth could tell she felt bad about all that had happened.

Now, Elizabeth was trying her hardest to be happy for her sister. She had only met Jack once at the rehearsal dinner, so maybe he was as great as Ellen claimed. It was her sister's track record that worried her. Ellen had gone on and on about the amazing attributes of Hannah's father too. She didn't know what it was about Ellen that caused her to feel so completely lost whenever she was alone.

"Ma'am?" Elizabeth turned to see a well-dressed man standing at her side. "They asked me to come and find you. Everyone's in the reception hall waiting for you to come so they can announce the bridal party."

Elizabeth couldn't stop staring at him. There wasn't anything in his appearance that would set him apart, but he had the most enchanting eyes. They were shadowed in hazel hues and seemed genuinely empathetic. "I'm sorry," she said, shaking her head and nervously shifting her bridesmaid bouquet into her left hand. "Do I know you?"

The man held out his hand. "Forgive me," he said. "My name is Connor Templeton. I'm the owner. Do you need a minute or can I usher you in?" She nodded as he gently wrapped her arm around his. "You look beautiful," he said, "and it's never a good idea to outshine the bride." He winked at her before leaving her with Ellen. For some reason, Elizabeth felt nervous.

The reception went as perfectly as Ellen had planned it. The food was the best they could afford, and while it wasn't dinner at the Ritz, she could tell her guests were pleased. Hannah looked lovingly elegant in her sparkling white flower girl dress, tied with a single lavender ribbon; her hair adorned with baby's breath. Her own dress was elegantly simple, fashion-forward, as her mother would say, and it fit her like a glove. She felt as if she were basking in the glow of a moment of happiness; trying to catch every memory and pin it in her mind. She couldn't remember the last time she'd felt simply content. Before she knew it, the DJ was announcing the last dance of the night, and the faithful few were gathering on the outside walk, bubbles in hand, waiting to wish the bride and groom farewell.

"You know," Elizabeth began as she helped her sister out of her wedding dress and into a flowery, layered sundress, "you deserve to be happy. You know I'm always here for you, no matter what."

"Oh, Lizzie," her sister said affectionately, the champagne and wine taking its full course, "you know I love you, too. And I am happy!" she beamed. Elizabeth hastily kissed her on the cheek and watched as she bounced down the walkway and climbed into the car with Jack, little Hannah peeking out from the backseat. She'd offered to take her for the weekend, but Jack had insisted they spend their time away as a family — Hannah included. Maybe *29* it was all going to be all right. Maybe this was the man of Ellen's dreams.

"It was a beautiful wedding, huh?" Elizabeth looked behind her and saw Connor. He was bending down to pick up a discarded plastic champagne glass. "I understand if you're tired, but, if not, I'd love to end the day with some hot coffee."

Elizabeth instinctively glanced down at her watch. He noticed and started to back off, picking up on her subtle hint. "It's just that I don't usually, I mean…" she sighed and bent down to remove her heels. " I am tired," she said, "and I haven't dated in a really long time, and it's been a crazy six months and…" she stopped and looked at him square in the face. She was losing her composure, probably coming across as a flighty little girl. "Will you promise me something?"

She could tell her question surprised him. "Look," he said, "I don't want you to think I'm in the habit of hooking up with people who come to this place. I'm sorry. It wasn't cool. I'll just go home, and you can go home, and we can pretend it never happened."

"You didn't answer my question," she said. "Will you promise me something?"

Connor matched her gaze. "Okay."

"Promise me I won't have regrets when this is done."

He walked over to her and took her shoes from her hands. "Let me carry those for you," he said. "It's been a long day and you look exhausted."

CHAPTER 7

"Elizabeth, you always want the impossible. I just can't make this happen overnight! Increase sales by 10%?"

Elizabeth looked at Tommy and smiled. "Oh, come on, Tom," she said. "This is our chance to increase our department's productivity, get the creative juices flowing, you know? Embrace a challenge! Conquer the world!" She was trying so hard to get him to laugh, to loosen up a bit. Tom only straightened and stuck his nose back down in his laptop. He sat there punching the keys before he looked up.

"I'll run the numbers one more time," he said, closing the lid. "But I'm not promising a miracle. I'm not freaking Mother Teresa!" Elizabeth couldn't help but chuckle at the overweight, chain-smoking middle-aged man in front of her. She definitely didn't need him to remind her of that! Tom may have looked a mess, but he was the best hire she had made in her three years at the company. If you could get beyond the stale cigarette smell, you would see an accounting genius... pocket protector, and all.

While Elizabeth was still talking to Tommy, her assistant said, "Mrs. Templeton?" Elizabeth glanced up at Sherry, who lowered her reading glasses and rubbed her eyes. "Your sister is here. Should I show her in?"

"Ellen?" Elizabeth asked. "Did she say what she needed?" Sherry shrugged her shoulders and shook her head. "Okay, yeah, go ahead and show her in." Elizabeth rearranged the documents on her desk and shuffled some papers into a pile. *What on earth does Ellen want?* She wondered. Instinctively, she reached for her purse and slipped it away in the drawer.

Tom quickly got up and tucked his laptop under his arm. "I'll let you know," he said, "but don't rush me!" He ran clumsily into Ellen on his way out and awkwardly stepped aside.

When Ellen walked through the door, Elizabeth couldn't help but smile. Poised and beautiful as usual, she had pulled her hair back into a loose ponytail with a fresh flower stuck in the band. Her light green summer dress flowed effortlessly around her. No matter what, Ellen was still and always would be the beauty of the family.

"Hi, Ellen," Elizabeth said. "I wasn't expecting to see you today. What's up?" Before Elizabeth knew what was happening, her sister sat down on the leather desk chair and started crying, her shoulders shaking. Elizabeth couldn't help but sigh. She had been here so many times with her sister in the years since she married Jack. "Let me guess," she said, handing her sister a tissue.

"It's Jack," Ellen said. "I just don't get him, Elizabeth. He's lost his job again. I don't know what to do this time, Lizzie. Honest to God, I don't know what to do! I just want to walk away, but then I think of Hannah, and what would she do if her daddy was just gone?"

"He's not her daddy, Ellen," Elizabeth corrected. "And maybe it's time to make a decision. Things haven't been right since the beginning. It's hard to see you keep trying and trying." Ellen was sobbing even louder now, and Elizabeth walked over and closed her office door. Sherry was peeking around her cubicle, trying to see what was going on. The last thing Elizabeth needed was more gossip about her family. "Ellen, you can't keep coming here when I'm working. I know you are having a hard time, but people start to talk and it's just not a good idea."

Ellen straightened up in her chair. "I'm sorry to be a bother, Lizzie. I'm sorry I thought I could come to my big-time successful sister when I needed advice and help. I'm sorry I thought… after all of those years of helping you… that I selfishly thought it was payback time!"

Elizabeth rushed over to her and laid a hand on her shoulder. "I didn't mean it like that!" she quickly said, glancing over her shoulder at the door. Her sister could go from zero to a hundred in a millisecond. Ellen's voice was escalating, and the walls in this place were thin as paper. "Just calm down, okay? Why don't you come over after work with Hannah? Connor would love to cook us all some dinner. He could grill or barbeque? —"

Ellen brushed off her hand and got up. "I can't. Jack said he wants to talk when I get home from work today." Elizabeth raised her eyebrows. "I told him I was at work. I just needed some time away from him today. Maybe some other time..." She placed her hand on the doorknob and then turned to look at Elizabeth once again. "I'm sorry, Lizzie. I'm sorry I keep coming here and bothering you. It's just ironic, you know? You were always the screw-up, and I was always the one that had it all together." With that, she turned the doorknob and left.

Elizabeth picked up a piece of paper off the desk and crumbled it in her hands. *Don't let her get to you*, she said to herself, then threw the paper as hard as she could through the open door. Connor, with impeccable timing, walked through the door and got hit square in the face with the crumbled ball of paper.

"I surrender!" he yelled and held up his hands. Lizzie couldn't help but laugh as she rushed over to her husband. He always knew when to show up. Connor brushed her hair from her eyes and pulled her towards him, one hand around her waist, the way she liked. "Hello, beautiful," he said gently kissing her.

"You just missed the firing squad," Elizabeth joked. "Ellen was here... same story, second verse same as the first."

"A little bit louder and a little bit worse?" Connor said sarcastically. "Sorry. How much does she need this time?"

"She didn't ask for anything, just complained, insulted me and left. I don't know what to do, Connor. It's as if she is mad at me for being successful. She's mad I finished school, married you, and got a job... found happiness. Sometimes I think she would be happier with her life if I were still stuck in that horrid tenement."

Connor shuddered and walked towards her desk. "That place was nasty," he said. "Remember that first night I dropped you off? I was afraid to walk in the door. I put you in front of me in case someone attacked. They'd get you first and I'd have time to run!"

"Ha, ha," Elizabeth said. "What are you here for, anyway? Don't you have an event to plan...A young, helpless woman to hit on at a wedding?"

"Ha, ha," Connor mocked. In a swift movement, he picked Lizzie up and *33* kissed her, long and passionately. "Frankly my dear," he said, "I'm here to pick you up from work. Or did you not realize it was already five o'clock?" Connor sat her down, but Lizzie didn't let go. She held his face in her hands and just stared, looking lovingly into his eyes. It had only been ten months since their wedding, nothing fancy. They had simply gone to the courthouse and said their vows in front of the judge. Elizabeth did not want the attention and Connor had been around too many weddings to even bother with a ceremony. Ellen, Hannah, and Connor's brother and parents were the only witnesses. Elizabeth had worn a simple, sleeveless white sheath and an old faded church hat of her mother's with a blush veil. She had never felt so beautiful.

"I love you, Connor," she said. "I really do." She quickly grabbed her things and turned off the light. Sherry had left a pile of messages in her inbox before she headed out. Elizabeth reached out to look at the pile, but Connor pulled her hand back as if to say, *it can wait*. "I'm craving barbeque chicken, Connor-style," she said.

"You know, most men have women that can cook. Connor do this, Connor do that," he said mockingly. "How I suffer for you!"

"Poor baby," Elizabeth consoled him. "Corn on the cob would be good, too. A real summer supper tipped off with a nice, big glass of red wine."

Connor laughed. "Wine, huh? That means you'll be asleep on the couch by eight o'clock."

Elizabeth sat back, trying to look shocked, "Asleep by eight, huh? Not if you play your cards right!" she teased and pinched his buttocks.

"Mrs. Templeton!" Connor yelled and jumped like a schoolgirl. "What would your mother say?" Elizabeth could only imagine. She knew Mama was smiling.

CHAPTER 8

"Connor, they'll be here any minute! Would you come and help me?" Elizabeth yelled down the hall. She was pacing back and forth from the walk-in closet to the bed, frantically holding dress after dress up in the mirror. Connor walked in with a bowl of ice cream, his sweats still on from his morning jog. "It's not even ten o'clock yet!" Elizabeth said, looking at him.

"Exactly! It's not even ten o'clock yet and you're already yelling like a lunatic. If a man wants to eat ice cream on his day off after running five miles, then he's allowed!" he said and shoved a spoonful of Rocky Road into his mouth.

"You're hopeless," Elizabeth teased and turned to go into the closet one last time. Before she could get away, Connor grabbed her and gave her an ice cream smeared kiss.

"That's for teasing me," he smiled and watched as she pouted away. "What's all the fuss about up here? Just pick a dress, you look good in anything."

"That was sweet, so I forgive you for the ice cream moustache," Elizabeth said. "Which dress should I wear? I've got this red one, but it's kind of late for the cool weather, or the purple one, but maybe that one's too heavy for this time of year?"

The doorbell rang and Connor gave her a quick kiss on the cheek. "Go with the red one," he said. "It makes your eyes go crazy," he yelled over his shoulder. Elizabeth could feel the gentle shake of the house as he bounced down the stairs and opened the door. She heard Connor jokingly offer everyone some ice cream and apologize for his appearance. Connor was always the peacemaker, the breaker-of-the-ice. Elizabeth hastily pulled the zipper up on her dress, slipped on a pair of simple sandals and went downstairs to see her family.

The staircase formed an "L" shape as it curved into the living room. When Lizzie rounded the corner, she gasped. She hadn't seen Hannah in months, and during that time, a transformation had occurred in the young girl. She was only 12 years old, but looking at her, you would guess much older. She had long, brown, silky hair that was naturally full and shiny. It had a slight wave and perfectly framed her rounded face. Her eyes were round and puppy-dog-like, just like her grandmother's. Elizabeth felt like she was looking at a picture of her mother; a younger version of the woman she loved so much.

"Aunt Liz!" Hannah yelled, running over to where Elizabeth was standing. Hannah pummeled her with a giant bear hug again, just like the comforting hugs their mother used to shower upon her daughters. Elizabeth squeezed her niece before stepping back to take a look at her.

"She's so pretty," she said over Hannah's head to Jack and Ellen. "All the little boys are gonna go crazy, huh?" she teased and lovingly pinched Hannah's cheeks. Hannah rolled her eyes and pulled away.

"Not my princess," Jack said and came over to Elizabeth. "Good to see you again," he said and reached out his hand to shake hers. He put his arm around Hannah's shoulder and kissed her on the head. "I'll scare all the boys away," he said and shifted his arm around her waist, pulling her even closer.

"Come on, Daddy," Hannah said. "What are you going to do? Lock me in a tower?" She walked into the kitchen and grabbed the bowl of ice cream Connor had made.

"Honestly, Connor," Ellen said. "It's only ten o'clock in the morning!"

"What is with you Carter women?" Connor retorted. "Anti ice cream? It's un-American! Besides, just let me be the fun uncle. Come on, Hannah," he said, "did you bring your swimsuit?" Hannah didn't need a second invitation. She ran towards the back door, stripping off garments as she ran; her Uncle Connor right behind her. On cue, they both cannon-balled into the pool and then raced to the other side.

"He's just a big kid," Elizabeth said to Ellen, "but he sure does enjoy life!" Elizabeth plugged in the coffee pot and turned the faucet on to fill up the tank.

Ellen cleared her throat and waited for Jack to exit through the back door, watching as he sat at the patio table. "Speaking of kids," she said, "any news?"

Elizabeth poured the coffee grounds on top of the filter and pressed the button to begin brewing. The smell of coffee soon filled the room. "Nothing yet. We're kind of at a crossroads. The doctors can't find anything wrong, but they can't find anything right, either. We're just taking some time to pray through it and see what to do next."

Ellen nodded her head and watched Hannah climb onto a giant blow-up frog in the pool. *At least I have Hannah,* she thought to herself. *You have your big house, but I have Hannah.* She slid her fingers across the granite countertop. The kitchen was surrounded with windows, and the natural light poured into the room; hitting the light yellow paint on the wall just right. The room reeked of happiness.

"I'm sorry about that," Ellen sympathized. Even she could hear her own insincerity. "Maybe when you stop trying you'll get pregnant. That's what they say happens."

"What about you and Jack?" Elizabeth asked. "Have you thought about having any more children?

"God, no!" Ellen replied without hesitation. "I mean, it's just that Hannah's already twelve and we're happy with just the one. Jack really doesn't want any more kids," she said, completely unaware of her insensitivity.

"I guess it's one of life's mysteries," Elizabeth said, "why people who want kids can't have them, and women who don't seem to care about their kids have no problem conceiving." Elizabeth knew it was a cheap shot, but she didn't care. It hadn't even been thirty minutes and they were already at each other.

"What's that supposed to mean?" Ellen said, crossing her arms. Luckily, for them both, Connor and Hannah came bursting through the back door, dripping water all over the hardwood floor.

"We should probably get the steaks on the grill," he said, smiling, looking back and forth at the two women. "Okay," he said and walked past them towards the refrigerator. "Here, Hannah, you take these out to the grill. I'll get the steak rub and be out in a minute." Hannah ran over to the grill and placed the steaks down. She was running towards the water when Jack called her over and sat her down on his lap.

"Okay, you two," Connor said. "I usually stay out of this, but it's a beautiful day, you just got here," he glanced at Ellen, "and today is about Hannah's birthday. Whatever you two have started, can it wait until later? Come outside and play," he said. "It'll make you feel better." He grabbed Elizabeth's hand and ushered her out to the back porch.

Ellen grabbed a coffee mug from the cabinet and poured herself a cup. Even her coffee tastes rich, she said to herself and reached in the fridge to pull out the creamer. She still needed to cool off and decided to walk through the front door and around to the back. As she rounded the corner, her eye caught a picture Elizabeth had placed on the mantle. It was that same old photograph of her mother and father, and sitting next to it was the teapot Elizabeth salvaged from the Goodwill pile so many years ago.

Ellen reached out and grabbed the picture. She noticed Elizabeth bought a new frame, but the teapot was still in the same beat-up condition. She gently touched her mother's face, without thinking, pulled the image towards her mouth, and kissed her mother's silhouette. She glanced around to make sure no one had seen her and put the picture back on the mantle.

"I like that one," Mama said, walking around Ellen in the dressing room. "It really is beautiful on you. Not too short and not too long, nice and modest." A young Ellen examined herself in the mirror.

"It's not too…" she hesitated to say the word, "cheap looking?" She glanced over at her mother's face and saw a sadness enter her eyes. "It's just that Penny's dress is from the department store and it looks so professional, you know? I just want to look nice."

Mama held her daughter's hand and helped her step down off the platform in the middle of the dressing room mirror. "We can't always afford niceness, honey, but it's the woman that makes the dress; the dress doesn't make the woman. A beautiful woman can make a cheap dress look like a ball gown." Ellen straightened up and glanced back toward the mirror. Mama always knew just what to say to make her feel so special.

Ellen remembered that prom night, so many years ago. She had worn the pastel pink dress so proudly as Ronny had come to pick her up. She couldn't wait to get to the dance and show it off. In true fashion, however, Ronny had quickly turned away from the school and headed toward the field outside of his parents' house. He pulled his truck behind a grove of trees, turned off the lights, and quickly started in on Ellen.

She remembered how she'd felt that night as he pulled her dress off and unbuckled his pants. He carelessly threw it under the driver's seat, and she watched, as it lay crumpled on the floor. She'd been wearing special undergarments to match her dress, and he didn't even notice. Like a dog in heat, he simply had his way and then stepped outside to smoke when he was done. Ellen remembered dressing behind the truck, coiffing her hair in the driver's side mirror. Ronny had looked at her from over the cigarette smoke. "You look pretty," he told her before they got in the truck and went into the dance.

That was the night Hannah was conceived almost twelve years ago to the day. She found out she was pregnant the day of graduation. She and Ronny weren't together anymore by then, and she never mentioned it to him. No matter how hard her mother tried to find out the name of the father, Ellen was firm. This was her child, no one else's.

As she rounded the fence into the backyard, she heard Elizabeth say, "Happy Birthday!" She must have handed Hannah a package because the girl ripped into it.

"Oh, my God, Aunt Lizzie!" she said as she turned to her mother. "Look, Mom, it's an iPod!" Ellen hugged her daughter.

"Say thank you, honey," she said curtly and watched as Hannah poured affection all over her aunt and uncle.

"Time for steaks!" Connor announced and began setting the table for lunch.

Ellen sat down next to Jack, whom she could tell felt as uncomfortable as she did. She asked Jack for a cigarette and lit up, taking puff after puff as Elizabeth passed plates and cold beers around the table. "I think I'll eat later," she said and unbuttoned her dress. She had worn a bright pink bikini for the pool and she caught Jack's eye as she dove into the deep end, 39 feeling the cool water rush over her flushed face. She swam over to the far edge of the pool and placed her elbows on the hot cement, her back towards the party.

CHAPTER 9

Hannah waved goodbye to her aunt and uncle as she climbed into her parents' old, rusted Honda Civic. She fastened her seatbelt and took out her iPod, holding the gadget tight in her hands. Her Uncle Connor had helped her download music, even paying for most of the songs to get her music library started. She put her headphones in her ears and leaned back on the seat, letting the music drown out her parents' voices in the front.

"That sure is a beautiful house," Ellen said casually, eyeing Jack.

"Don't start, Ellen," Jack replied. "Not tonight."

"I'm just saying it's beautiful, is all. And that pool! It sure would be nice to have a house even half that size, or even to have a house," she said, keeping her eyes straight ahead.

"Ellen," he said in a warning tone. "Leave it."

"What?" she said innocently. "Can I help it if I'm tired of living in an apartment and I'm ready for a home with an actual garage, Jack? It's been twelve years since we got married. I just thought by now we'd be… —"

"It's never good enough for you, is it?" Jack interrupted. "No matter what I do, how hard I work, it's never good enough!"

Ellen laughed, "Work?" she said. "Since when have you worked? Last time I checked, my paycheck was the one keeping us above water. We're never going to get ahead, Jack, never. Is this really the way you want to raise Hannah? In an apartment, never having a home to call our own?"

Jack sighed and leaned his elbow on the window, letting the cool summer night air drift through the car. "Stupid woman," he said. "You always knew how to ruin a good day. What do you want me to say? I provide the best I know how, and if that's not good enough, then… "He stopped short and fumbled with a cigarette in his pocket, lighting it up as they stopped at the red light. " Face it, Ellen, this is your paradise, and you don't have nowhere else to go." He looked over at her and blew the smoke in her direction, his large frame looming over her, daring her to continue.

Ellen opened the door to the car and jumped out onto the curb. "I'm sick of this, of all of this!" she said, motioning to the car. "Go on!" she yelled at him as the light turned green. "Leave me!"

"Woman, are you crazy?" Jack yelled. "Get in the car, now!" Hannah had taken her earplugs out now and was watching her mother, her eyes full of fright. Ellen started running down the pavement. "Fine!" screamed Jack and sped off.

"Daddy!" Hannah yelled. "What're you doing? You can't just leave her! Back up and pick her up!" Jack faced forward, his face as stone cold as the pavement Ellen was sobbing into. "Daddy!" Hannah yelled louder. "Stop!"

Jack slammed on the brakes and got out of the car. He walked back to Ellen and picked her up. "Get in the car!" he yelled and dragged her back to the Civic. Ellen crumpled into the front seat and started sobbing, not even trying to hide her tears from her daughter. They drove the rest of the way in deafening silence until they pulled up to their apartment building and Ellen stormed inside, leaving Jack and Hannah in the car.

Inside the apartment, Hannah glanced at the table and saw remnants of the birthday cake left from this morning when her mother had surprised her with an early birthday treat. They had sat on her bed and dug into the chocolate cake, laughing and talking about her birthday. It was a special treat her mother had done every year that Hannah could remember. She told Hannah that life was too short to wait until dinner to have your birthday cake.

They talked and laughed, Hannah speculating that nobody else in the world probably got birthday cake before they had even brushed their teeth. Her mother had made her favorite cake in the world, German Chocolate, and allowed her to eat as much as she desired. Even though she left for her aunt's house feeling a little sick from the sugar, she wouldn't have traded the morning for anything. "Happy birthday to me," Hannah muttered and walked into her room. She'd forgotten her mother had painted a big "12" on the door in sparkly gold puffy paint, the kind that you peel off when it dries. Hannah didn't feel like removing the paint; the truth was she wished her birthday would just end. She almost felt guilty for turning 12 at all and making her mother face her Aunt Elizabeth. She knew their life was different than her aunt's. She just couldn't figure out why it made her mother so sad.

"Come in," Hannah said as she heard a knock on the door. Ellen timidly opened the door and looked in on Hannah.

"I'm going out for a little bit, baby," she said. "You'll probably be asleep when I come in, so I'll see you tomorrow."

As she turned to leave, Hannah called out, "Thanks for the cake, mom." Ellen turned around, and Hannah could see tears forming in her mother's eyes. All she could do was nod at her daughter, biting her lower lip to keep from crying once again. When Hannah heard the front door close, she walked out into the living room where Jack was sitting on the couch, watching TV.

"Why do you and Mom always fuss?" she asked as she snuggled next to him on the couch. He smelled like beer and sweat, both mixing in with the musty smell sunk into the lining of the old couch. "Do you and Mommy even love each other anymore?" Jack turned away from the TV and lovingly brushed her bangs out of her eyes. "Well, I love you, Daddy," Hannah said.

Jack took a sip of his beer. "I love you, too, princess," he said looking back at the TV. Hannah turned to the TV and for the first time noticed what her stepfather was watching. The couple in the show began tearing into each other, ripping off their clothes and breathing heavily. The man pushed the woman back against the wall and held her hands above her head as he kissed his way down her chest and over her stomach. Hannah sat mesmerized as the camera panned directly over the woman's breasts, hiding nothing from the audience.

"Daddy, what are they doing?" Hannah asked as the man unbuttoned his pants and started pressing himself into the woman. This time the camera zoomed in, focusing on the man's buttocks as he moved up and down on the woman.

Jack turned to face her. "When two people love each other, that's what they do princess." Confused, she nodded her head and looked back at the TV. "Do you love me?" he asked.

Hannah backed away a little from him on the couch. She started to feel funny on the inside and wished her stepfather would turn the channel. "Yes, Daddy," she said, looking down at her iPod. She'd just started to get up off the couch when Jack pulled her back down and passionately kissed her. Hannah could feel her stepfather's tongue slide into her mouth and she pushed him away. She covered her mouth with her hand as the aftertaste of beer clung to her tongue.

"See how much Daddy loves you, too?" Hannah looked at Jack, confused. As Jack turned back to the TV, Hannah watched the front door, wishing her mother would come home soon. Clutching her iPod, she walked into her room and closed the door, leaving Jack in the living room watching TV.

Hannah changed into her pajamas and curled up on the bed, listening for the front door to open, waiting to hear her mother return. She looked at the clock as it passed midnight and finally the weight of the day forced her eyes closed. She fell asleep, huddled in a small ball at the top of her bed.

CHAPTER 10

The smell of bacon filled the small apartment and woke Hannah up before her alarm went off for school. Still feeling groggy, she crawled out of bed and into the bathroom. Her mouth tasted horrible. She'd forgotten to brush her teeth last night and the rancid taste of alcohol left a filmy presence on the roof of her mouth. Grabbing her toothbrush, she brushed her teeth, tongue, and mouth until it all felt numb from the bristles.

She turned the hot water knob all the way, waiting for the hot steam to fill the bathroom and wash her young silhouette. As the water ran down, she couldn't help but play through the events of last night. Her mind drifted to her aunt's house, the barbeque, and the pool. She remembered how good it felt just to be around her Aunt Liz and her Uncle Connor. They always seemed so in love, so happy. They lived on the good side of town; the side of town her classmates made fun of. But Hannah had promised herself long ago she would one day live by her aunt. At the beginning of last summer when she visited her aunt, the house next door was for sale. Hannah begged her mother to schedule a walk-through with the realtor. Hannah soaked it all in: the luxurious bathrooms, the soft, foamy carpeting. She closed her eyes in the middle of the kitchen, imagining how she would decorate, visualizing herself living in such extravagance.

"Morning, baby," Ellen said as Hannah sunk into the kitchen table chair. Ellen yawned as she plated the eggs and bacon and sat them on the table. Jack came into the kitchen and put his hands on Hannah's shoulders, softly rubbed her back and kissed her neck. Hannah couldn't help but stiffen at the usual welcome gesture. "Good morning, princess," he said and walked over to the counter to pour a cup of coffee.

Ellen was leaning against the countertop, still yawning and rubbing her 45 bloodshot eyes with the back of her hand. Hannah noticed her mother looked slightly disheveled, not her usual put-together self. She had on her work clothes, but it all looked thrown together, not carefully picked out and placed. Ellen looked at her watch. "Come on, Hannah. Finish breakfast and let's get going. You've got school today."

"I'll take her," Jack said. Hannah glanced over at him and saw him shove a spoonful of eggs into his mouth. Ellen raised her eyebrows and glared at him from over her coffee mug. "What?" he asked her.

"Are you sure?" Ellen asked. She couldn't remember the last time Jack volunteered to do anything.

"She's my daughter, too," he grumbled as he tore off a piece of bacon.

"Don't let her be late," Ellen said as she kissed Hannah on the cheek and grabbed her purse. "Here's some lunch money, Hannah," Ellen said, shoving a five-dollar bill into her hands. "And don't take your iPod to school!" she yelled over her back as she grabbed her keys and closed the front door behind her.

She didn't know why, but Hannah felt nervous as she sat across from her stepfather. She reached out to take a sip of her juice and her hands slipped, spilling the juice all down the front of her shirt.

"Hurry on and change," Jack said. "We can't be late."

Hannah walked into her room and fumbled in her drawers for a new blouse. The one she had on was a birthday present from her mother, and the color really made her complexion pop. *I'm so silly*, she said to herself as she looked for a matching shirt. Ripping the buttons apart, she stood in front of her dresser in her bra as she started to put on the new shirt. Most of the girls in her class were still in training bras, but Hannah had developed early. Her mother had taken her to the department store months ago to find *a real bra; the kind a woman wears*, she had said. As she was slipping the shirt over her head, she glanced in her dresser mirror and saw Jack standing in the doorway, smiling at her over his coffee.

"What are you doing, Daddy?" she gasped, holding her arms up to hide her chest. Hannah watched in the mirror as he sat his coffee cup down on her bedside table and sat on the bed, her pink gingham comforter still a mess from this morning.

come back after she left us," he said, glancing over at his stepdaughter. "Do you want Mommy and Daddy to fight?" he asked her.

All of a sudden, Hannah thought of Dodger, the old greyhound that lived in the first floor apartment. His owner, Mr. Sams, treated him so bad that Dodger would cower when anyone else would approach him. She remembered playing in the back of the apartment building when she was little and seeing Mr. Sams slap Dodger with the back of his hand for spilling his food bowl. Even as a little girl, she thought it was weird that Dodger never fought back. He would just slink back into the corner, shaking like he was a puppy. "I don't want you to fight," Hannah said, looking towards the school.

"Alright, then, give Daddy a kiss," he said and pulled her towards him. Hannah almost threw up in his mouth as once again he slid his tongue into her mouth, lingering for a few seconds as Hannah sat motionless in the passenger seat. "Go on, then," he said.

Hannah opened the car door and stepped out, her knees feeling weak as her feet hit the pavement. She fumbled for her schoolbag on the floor and slammed the door shut. For the first time in her life, she couldn't get into the building fast enough.

CHAPTER 11

"Sherry, where's that report from marketing?" Elizabeth shuffled papers around on her desk, flinging items here and there, creating even more piles as she looked for the bright red folder.

Sherry popped her head in the office door. "The one in the red folder?" she asked. Elizabeth nodded without looking up, quickly picking up a stack of papers from under her desk, and thumbing through it.

"The meeting is in ten minutes, Sherry," said Elizabeth, "and I can't find it. I know I read it and I remember what it says, but I just can't find it."

"Found it!" Sherry held the folder over her head triumphantly. "You know, you really don't pay me enough, Liz." She smiled as she handed Liz the folder. The phone rang and Sherry picked it up instinctively. "Liz Templeton's office," she said sweetly. "One moment." She handed the receiver to Elizabeth and walked out. "It's your niece," she called back.

"My niece?" Elizabeth muttered. "H-hello?" There was silence on the other line as Elizabeth waited. "Hello? Hannah, are you there?"

"Sorry to bother you at work, Aunt Liz." She sounded like she'd been crying, her voice barely audible in the receiver.

Elizabeth immediately sat down. "What's wrong, Hannah? Are you okay? Are you hurt?"

"No, no, nothing like that," she reassured her aunt. "I'm just not feeling well and I can't get a hold of my mom. Do you think you could pick me up from school? They won't let me leave and walk home by myself — I have to have an adult." Elizabeth looked at the clock, and then glanced at the folder in her hands.

"Of course," she said. "I'll leave as soon as I can and come straight there. Do you need to go to the doctor? Should I make an appointment?"

Hannah's voice changed. "No, I'm not that sick. I just need to rest is all," she insisted, "Thanks, Aunt Liz. I'll be out front waiting."

Elizabeth gathered her purse and jacket and placed the red folder in her briefcase. "Sherry, tell Vic I'm sorry, but I can't make the meeting." Sherry raised her eyebrows. "I know what he's going to say, but he'll just have to deal with it. It's not the end of the world. Tell him I should be available tomorrow and rearrange the schedule to accommodate him." Sherry pursed her lips and opened her desktop calendar. "It's nothing serious — my niece is just not feeling well and my sister can't get off work."

Sherry nodded and took a sip of coffee. "Whatever you say, boss," she said. "I'll tell Vic. I hope she feels better." Elizabeth walked past the corridors of cubicles and into the elevator. There was something about her niece that didn't seem right. In all her years at school, Hannah had never called her to come and get her. Elizabeth actually couldn't remember a single time when Hannah had been sick enough to miss school. And she didn't sound sick, either. She just sounded sad. *Probably just a fight with a friend or something,* Elizabeth thought and opened the car door.

When Elizabeth pulled up to the school, Hannah was waiting outside with the school nurse. Elizabeth stepped out of the car and started walking towards Hannah. Her shoulders were slumped and her long, beautiful hair looked greasy, unkempt. For a young girl who was always as polished and pristine as her mother, Elizabeth couldn't help but notice that she was wearing a simple t-shirt and jeans and one of her sneakers wasn't even tied. Her entire appearance seemed distracted.

"You must be Hannah's aunt," the nurse said and shook her hand. "She doesn't have a fever, but she says her stomach hurts so I think it's best to send her home. There are only a few classes left in the day, anyway." The nurse looked at Hannah. "I'll call you tonight to make sure you are feeling better," she said and walked inside. Elizabeth grabbed Hannah's bag and placed it in the backseat. She opened the car door for the young girl and watched as she fastened her safety belt and slumped down in the seat.

"I don't want you to be home by yourself right now," Elizabeth said, "so I'll just take you to our house, okay?" Hannah didn't say anything but simply nodded. She reached a hand to her face and Elizabeth thought she saw her wiping away a tear. Elizabeth reached into her coat pocket and pulled out her cell phone. She had left her Bluetooth earpiece on her desk, so she tried to punch in the number for Connor while keeping her eyes on the road.

The morning fog had never entirely lifted, and now there was a slight drizzle falling around them. The car swerved a little bit as she pressed the call button on her phone and waited for Connor to answer. "Liz?" he said. "What's up?"

Elizabeth glanced over at Hannah and tried to make her voice deceptively cheerful. "Hey, Hannah wasn't feeling well so I just picked her up from school. She's just coming to our house until Ellen gets off work and can pick her up."

"Tell her I'll pick something up for dinner, whatever she wants," said Connor, "and don't worry about our date tonight — we can reschedule."

Elizabeth smiled. "Thanks, Con," she said affectionately. "I love you. I'll see you later." The phone conversation ended and Elizabeth once again tried to engage Hannah in conversation. "Connor said he would bring home your favorite dinner," she said. "What should I tell him to get?" Hannah shifted in her chair and pushed her hair behind her ears.

"I don't care, Aunt Liz. It really doesn't matter," she said.

"How about Italian then?" said Liz and handed the phone to Hannah. "Do you mind texting your uncle for me? Just tell him to pick up Pizanos. He's good at figuring out what people will like, so I'm sure he'll get something perfect for you." Hannah reached out a hand without looking and grabbed the phone. In seconds, she had sent her Uncle Connor the message, right as they were pulling into the garage. Elizabeth reached into the backseat and grabbed her briefcase, her purse, and Hannah's bag. With full arms, she opened the door into the kitchen and plopped everything onto the table. Hannah came in behind Liz and closed the door.

Elizabeth walked over to her niece and gave her a hug. "Do you want to go and lie down?" she asked. "You can take our bed or you can use the spare bedroom down the hall." Hannah shook her head and looked up at her aunt. "Yes?" asked Elizabeth.

"I just…" she said slowly. "I mean, there was something I wanted to ask you." Her voice was faltering and Elizabeth reached a hand out to push her hair from her face.

"Hannah, is there something you want to talk about? You don't feel sick, do you?" Hannah pushed her palms against her face, wiping the tears away abruptly.

"I just wanted to ask if I could take a shower is all," she said. Elizabeth nodded and gave her another hug.

"You know you can always talk to me, Hannah," she said. "The towels are in the closet in the bathroom and feel free to use anything else in there you need."

Elizabeth could hear the water running and started up a pot of coffee. It was just a little past two o'clock in the afternoon. She waited until she knew Hannah was in the shower and then dialed Ellen's number on her phone. "Hello?" a voice said on the other end.

"May I speak to Ellen, please?" said Elizabeth and waited for her sister to pick up.

"Hello?" said Ellen, sounding tired.

"Hey, sis," said Elizabeth. "I have Hannah. She's at Connor's and my place. Are you coming by after work?"

"What do you mean you have Hannah?" asked Ellen. "Why isn't she at school? Is everything okay?"

Elizabeth was taken aback. "Oh," she said, "I thought you knew. Hannah called me sick from school to come and pick her up. I just assumed she had called you, too," she said, trying to dispel any discomfort her sister might have felt.

Ellen paused. "No, she didn't call," she finally said and sighed. "I just agreed to work a double shift so I'll have Jack stop by on his way home from work," she said.

Elizabeth thought she would try one more question. "Ellen, have you noticed anything unu—"

Ellen interrupted Elizabeth. "Sorry, Lizzie," she said, "I have to get back to work. I'll tell Jack and talk to you later." The phone clicked and Elizabeth stood in the kitchen, staring at the receiver. Ellen was working too many double shifts lately, and it seemed like she was always tired and in a hurry. She had said Jack would be coming from work, but Elizabeth hadn't realized he was employed again. Last time they talked, Jack was between jobs yet again and Ellen was in her usual state of frustration.

Hannah walked into the room, her hair wet and matted to her young face. "I just spoke with your mom," she said. Hannah's head jerked up quickly but she said nothing. "She has to work a double shift tonight," she said. "She said she'll send Jack to pick you up." Elizabeth wasn't sure if she had imagined it, but it seemed like Hannah's entire body tensed. "I'm sorry I called your mom," she said quickly. "I must have misunderstood you in the car," she said, trying to give Hannah the benefit of the doubt.

"I'm not feeling so well, Aunt Liz," said Hannah. "Do you mind if I go ahead and lie down?" Elizabeth walked with Hannah and pulled back the covers of the guest bed. She tucked Hannah in and kissed her on the forehead, turning the ceiling fan on as she left to give the young girl a cool breeze while she was sleeping.

It had been a month since the barbeque, but Hannah seemed different. Elizabeth could tell something was bothering her, but she didn't want to push her niece. She tried to think of what her mother would have done if she was alive, and the pang of remorse quickly fluttered across her. Back in the kitchen, she poured herself a cup of coffee and took out her laptop, trying to get some work done before Connor came home.

When Connor finally did make it in, he was laden with takeout bags from Pizanos. The grease from the mozzarella sticks was oozing through the bag as he pulled out spaghetti with meatballs, spinach lasagna, breadsticks, and three individually sized portions of tiramisu for dessert. He kissed Elizabeth on the cheek. "Where is she?" he asked.

Elizabeth nodded towards the guest room, saying, "She's been asleep for almost an hour."

Connor walked over to the fridge and pulled out a bottle of water. "Hopefully she'll feel better when she wakes up," he said and sat down at the table with Liz. He had stopped at the mailbox on the way in and was thumbing through a good-sized pile of bills, magazines, junk mail, and coupon mailers. "Is Ellen coming?"

Elizabeth shut the lid to her laptop. "No, Jack is coming," she said, "from work." She glanced over at Connor, who looked up.

"Miracles can happen," he said jokingly.

"Connor, I'm not so sure Hannah is sick. Something else seems wrong. I can't pinpoint it, but she seems different, like something's happened that she's ashamed to admit."

Connor set the mail aside and cleared his throat. "It's probably just some school drama. I wouldn't worry too much. She seemed fine at the barbeque last month," he said. Out of the corner of his eye, he saw Hannah walk into the kitchen. "She's alive!" he said triumphantly and rose to give her a hug. "Here you go m'lady. Let the feast begin!" Walking over to the drawer at the left of the stove, he pulled out three forks. Elizabeth got up and pulled a two-liter of soda from the fridge, grabbed three cups and placed them on the table.

"Should I get the plates?" offered Hannah. "Paper or regular?"

"Oh, nothing but the fine china for you," said Connor and threw a stack of paper plates in her direction. Hannah wasn't prepared for the toss and dropped the plates on the ground. "Crap!" she sputtered. "I'm so sorry, Uncle Connor, I wasn't ready." She hurriedly gathered the plates together and Connor bent down to help.

"No worries," he said gently and gathered them up. "I should have given you advance warning. Sometimes I don't know my own strength," he winked at her and sat down next to Liz. Just as he began spooning the lasagna onto the plates, the doorbell rang. Hannah's head jerked up once again.

"I'll get it," said Elizabeth and walked to the front door. When she opened the door, Jack was standing in the doorway, looking awkward. "Jack," she said, "I haven't seen you in a while. Connor just brought some dinner home. Do you want to join us?"

"No," Jack said without hesitation. "I mean, thank you, but I need to get going. Hannah?" he yelled into the house without stepping beyond the front stoop. Within a few minutes, Hannah was at the door with her backpack slung over one shoulder.

"Sorry about dinner, Aunt Lizzie," she said and gave her aunt a quick hug

As she pulled away, Elizabeth pulled her in tighter, whispered in her ear, "I hope you feel better," and gave her a quick kiss on the cheek.

Hannah walked quickly down the sidewalk and got into the car. She held her breath, waiting as Jack wrestled his seat belt over his beer gut and started the engine. "You didn't, uh," he said cautiously, "tell Aunt Elizabeth about our secret, did you?"

"No," said Hannah, holding her backpack against her chest.

"Good," he said, relaxing and putting the car in drive. "You did good. It's our little secret, Hannah." She nodded and bit her lip, fighting back the tears. Hannah kept staring forward throughout the drive home, wishing it would somehow miraculously take hours to get to their apartment. When Jack pulled into the apartment complex, he parked a little ways from the door and watched as Hannah jumped out of the car before the engine had even been turned off. She arrived at the door ahead of Jack and reached into her pocket for the keys. She sighed. She had left her apartment keys in her locker at school. When she went in to see the nurse, she had never gone back to her locker to get her purse. She waited for Jack to catch up and unlock the door. They made their way up to the second floor, Jack leading and Hannah trailing behind.

Inside the apartment, Hannah dropped her backpack on the floor and headed towards her bedroom. "Hannah?" Jack called. She froze in the hallway and turned around. He walked over to her and slid his right hand under her shirt. "Since you don't feel good," he said slowly as he smiled down at her, "let me make you feel better." Hannah swallowed and looked away, closing her eyes as he fumbled with her pants. She bit her lip as he slowly lifted her shirt over her head and lowered her down onto the hallway floor. This time he didn't bother holding her hands as he kissed her breasts, moved down towards her navel and then began to molest her once again. He wrapped her legs around his neck and pushed them hard upwards as his hands began to caress her.

Hannah closed her eyes and imagined sitting down with her aunt and uncle, finishing the last bites of tiramisu, her favorite dessert. She imagined they must be laughing and talking at dinner. They seemed so far away.   *55*

Angela Hood & Daphne Cayo

CHAPTER 12

The night air felt cool as Elizabeth stood at the door and watched the car pull Jack and Hannah away. Her mind was swirling from the events of the last few hours and her feet were aching from the long day at work when she finally walked to sit down on the front stoop. Something isn't right, she said to herself and found herself wishing she had done a better job at keeping in contact with Hannah since she and Connor had married. It seemed like overnight her niece had transformed from a little girl into a young woman, and it was happening too fast for Elizabeth to fully comprehend.

As she sat on the cool concrete, her mind drifted back to her own child-hood. Unlike Hannah, she had been awkward, all legs and no roundness at all gangly and skinny. She hadn't even started her period until her junior year in high school, so different from her sister Ellen. Elizabeth's idea of a good time was sitting at home with her mother, where Ellen couldn't seem to get out of the house fast enough on a Friday night. As she thought of her mother, she felt sorry her niece would never know such a beautiful woman; the glue that always managed to hold her own and everyone else's lives together.

"Mama," Elizabeth spoke into the night air, "I still miss you so much." She closed her eyes as a breeze blew around the porch, causing chill bumps to rise on her skin.

Rose looked at her daughter from across the room and smiled. As usual, Elizabeth was curled up on the old easy chair, book in hand, mind closed to the world around her, and enthralled in the one found in the pages of her book. That chair had belonged to the girls' father; the one thing he had contributed to their apartment when they first married. The day he left, he 57 got up from that chair and walked out; taking with him the small suitcase, he had already packed. Rose tried to get rid of it on several occasions, but it was always the one thing of his she could never let go of. Elizabeth looked so much like him.

She walked over to where her daughter was sitting and looked at the cover of the book. "Oh, I always wanted to read that one," she said, pushing her daughter's bangs out of her eyes. She turned on the floor lamp. "You'll go blind reading in the dark, baby girl," she said.

Elizabeth rolled her eyes. "Oh, Mama," she said, "That's just an old wives' tale." She turned her attention once more back into Jane Austen's *Pride and Prejudice.*

"Are you reading for school?" Rose asked as she sat the grocery bags down in the kitchen. She heard the soft thump of the book closing and waited for Ellen to appear in the doorway.

"Yeah, for English class. You would like it, I think," she said and started pulling out various items from the bags. She rummaged around for something convenient and edible and settled upon a box of cheese crackers. "It's all love and romance."

Rose chuckled, "Oh, baby girl," she said, "I've had enough of both to last me a lifetime." She sighed and grabbed the box from her daughter. "And it's too close to dinner for this," she said, setting the box in the cupboard. Elizabeth jumped up onto the counter and pulled her long, skinny legs up to her flat chest. She caught a glimpse of herself in the reflection from the microwave and quickly looked away.

"Mama?" she asked.

"Hmm?" Rose answered as she filled the stew pot with water.

"Do you think some people are destined to find love while others are destined to be alone?" Rose turned off the water and looked at her daughter long and hard before she spoke. She knew she wasn't supposed to have favorites with her children, but she had always felt an affinity toward Elizabeth. Perhaps it was the underdog factor. Ever since she could remember she sought out those on the lower end of the spectrum in life, including the girls' father. He was about as underdog as you could get. Rose sat the pot of water on the stove and lit the pilot light.

"You know," she said, "a shallow love can come quickly, but those that have to wait for love get the blessing of depth, which is better than the joy of width." She placed her hands on her daughter's knees. "I don't think you have to worry," she said affectionately. "God's too good to leave you all alone in life." She kissed her daughter on the forehead and went back to making dinner.

❦

Elizabeth jumped. She had been thinking so deeply about her mother she hadn't even heard Connor walk outside and sit on the step above her. He wrapped his arms around hers and his head was resting on her shoulder. "That's a lot of food for one man," he said. Elizabeth turned her head and gave him a quick kiss.

"Sorry, Con," she said. "I was just thinking about Hannah. Did she seem okay to you tonight?"

Connor drew her closer in, wrapping his legs around hers. She was glad for the warmth emanating from his body. "There you go again," he said, "over thinking."

Elizabeth nodded and intertwined her left hand into his. Connor was probably right. She was always making things into too big of a deal; rethinking and rehashing every little detail of life until her own brain grew tired.

Connor went on, "She seemed distracted, but I pegged that to just being sick. She's almost a teenage girl, Elizabeth. She'll be up one day and down the next. Just be there for her, you know?"

Elizabeth felt in her pocket for her cell phone and contemplated calling Ellen. She knew her sister was at work, but something inside of her just didn't feel right. Her mother had always told her she had the gift of prophecy; Ellen had simply called her a pessimist. Dropping her cell phone back in her pocket, her body quivered from the chill of the night. "Let's go eat," she said, standing up and holding her hand out for Connor. "I could use a big glass of wine tonight." Together, they walked inside.

Angela Hood & Daphne Cayo

CHAPTER 13

Ellen lifted herself from the bed, her head pounding from a lack of sleep. She had pulled a double shift again at the hospital, and when she came home last night, Jack was in the mood. It took all of her strength to muster up even the faintest amount of interest, but Jack didn't seem to mind. He was still sleeping soundly next to her, his snores filling the bedroom. Rubbing her eyes, she forced her legs to swing off the bed and looked at the clock.

"Jack!" she said, pushing him on the arm, "Jack, get up. We're late. It's already 11:30 and we have to be there by noon." Jack mumbled and looked at her, eyes half open. "Elizabeth's house," she said, "for the barbeque. Come on. Get up." She swung on her bathrobe that was lying on the floor next to the bed and walked into the hallway. She nearly ran into Hannah, who had just come from her own room. She was carrying a large duffel bag with her change of clothes and makeup, already thinking of swimming in her aunt's pool.

"Morning," Ellen said and turned on the bathroom light. "You should have woken us," she told her daughter. "We're going to be late."

"I figured," said Hannah. "You hate going to Aunt Liz's house. I know you do." Ellen looked at her daughter, still trying to fight off the drowsiness. Sometime over the last school year, Hannah had changed. She'd quit giving her the respect she once did, but Ellen was too tired and too distracted by work to really take notice.

"Let's try to be nice," she said to her daughter. "At least give me ten minutes before you get sassy with me." Hannah rolled her eyes and sat down on the couch in the front room.

The car ride to Elizabeth and Connor's was spent in silence. Ellen had already yelled at Jack for rolling out of bed and getting in the car; he looked a total mess. His hair was unkempt, highlighting his receding hairline. He hadn't even bothered to brush his teeth and he still smelled of sweat from the factory. Hannah was in the backseat, her headphones in her ears and her eyes looking out the window taking in the changing scenery as they left her neighborhood and headed to her aunt's house.

When they pulled up to the house, Ellen noticed the balloons and signs that covered the front lawn. "Finally a teenager!" said one, and "Happy Birthday, Hannah!" said another. In the craziness of the morning, Ellen had completely forgotten her daughter's birthday. She felt to say anything at this point was useless; the damage had been done. Hannah opened the backseat door before Jack had even stopped the car and bounced up the front steps. Ellen could see her orange bikini straps cradling her thin shoulders, sticking out from the halter-top she wore over her swimsuit. Before Hannah could even ring the doorbell, Elizabeth opened the door and gave her niece a big hug. She waved toward Ellen and Jack in the car and turned to go inside with Hannah.

"Please be civil today," Ellen said to Jack, who was smoking the last few puffs of his cigarette before he tossed it out the window. "Just get through this."

Jack blew the smoke towards her. "I'll be on my best behavior," he said unconvincingly. "At least I'll get free barbeque and beer out of this."

Ellen rolled her eyes and slammed the door as hard as she could. She immediately noticed the small mound of presents as she walked in the front door. Hannah and Elizabeth were hunched over something in the kitchen and Ellen walked over to the pair, almost feeling like an intruder in her daughter's happiness. She always became elated around her aunt and uncle.

"It's awesome, Aunt Liz," said Hannah. "This is exactly what I wanted, and chocolate chip cheesecake is my favorite!" Ellen looked down at the table and saw The Cheesecake Factory box, the lid opened to reveal a full-size cheesecake.

"Oh, Elizabeth," she said, "you didn't have to get that. It's too much. You know a cake would have been just fine." She caught Hannah's glare.

The young girl deliberately kissed and hugged her aunt in front of her mother. "This is going to be the best birthday ever," she said to her aunt. "Where's Uncle Connor?"

"Out back as usual, manning the grill. Go ahead. I know you can't wait to get your swimsuit wet!" As Hannah went out the back door onto the patio, Ellen turned to her sister.

"You can just stop it, Elizabeth," she said hotly.

Elizabeth looked shocked. "Stop what?" she asked, confused. "What are you talking about?"

"Just because you can't have kids doesn't mean you can steal mine. No matter how many presents you give her, how many fancy cakes you buy, she'll never be your daughter. Face it, Hannah is mine, and that's that." She folded her arms and looked at her sister. She felt a sick sense of happiness from the unprovoked attack.

Elizabeth lowered her eyes and looked down at the table. "I know you forgot her birthday, Ellen. And, no offense, but if this is a competition, you don't exactly win mother of the year," Elizabeth was surprised at her own confidence. "I'll see you on the back porch," she said, and, balancing the cheesecake, opened the back door with one hand and walked outside.

The simple barbeque ended with a mound of watermelon rinds, half-eaten potato chip bags, and empty beer bottles. Elizabeth was watching Hannah do laps in the pool; envious of her youthful ability to down a huge amount of food and still have the ability to go swimming. She felt like she would be sick if she even attempted to get in the water. She glanced over at her sister. Ellen had been cordial throughout the meal, yet managed to speak around Elizabeth, never straight at her. Elizabeth still couldn't figure out what made her sister so angry whenever they were together.

Jack and Connor were talking about something on their own. Elizabeth was just grateful Connor was making an attempt. She knew Jack wasn't the easiest guy to have around. He had already helped himself to plenty of beer and had single-handedly downed most of the barbeque and eaten more than his share of the cheesecake. Any trace of the man that had originally wooed Ellen was no longer visible. He was starting to look old. Ellen, however, was still as ravishing as she was eight years ago when they married, if not more so. Just like their mother, she was aging beautifully.

Elizabeth watched Hannah get out of the pool, heaving her body over the edge with the ease of youth. As she walked towards Ellen, her eye caught a small butterfly on the girl's ankle, "Hey!" Elizabeth called out, "What's that?" she said, pointing at the butterfly. Hannah shrugged her shoulders and kissed her mother's cheek.

"Why don't you ask her, Aunt Liz?" she said and laughed. "That one almost got me disowned. I'm going inside to change," she announced and slipped away. Elizabeth looked at Ellen.

"She did it one day at the mall, without my permission," Ellen said. Elizabeth sat and pondered whether or not she should broach the subject further with her sister. With tensions already high, she decided to let it go. She started clearing the table as Jack walked past her into the house.

Hannah reached into the linen closet in the bathroom and pulled out a towel. She liked the way her aunt's towels felt, supple and lush, not threadbare like the cheap discount store ones her mother bought. Flipping her hair over her head, she used the towel to stop the drips from falling off the ends. She slipped out of her two-piece and wrapped the towel around her, ringing the swimsuit pieces in the sink; trying to get out every last drop of water before hanging them over the tub. She reached into the shower and turned the water on, waiting as the hot water began to flow and slowly filled the room with steam. She reached her hand over to turn on the bathroom fan when the door slowly opened. "Someone's in…" She called out and stopped when she saw Jack's face. She stood frozen, her hand clutching the towel. *Surely he won't do this today*, she said to herself, *not while everyone is here.* As he walked towards her, she hoped to God he would only try for a kiss. He stopped suddenly and turned around, locking the door.

For a split second, Hannah felt like screaming and then stopped herself. *How stupid could I have been to leave the door open?* "Jack," she begged, "please."

Jack walked towards her and unwrapped the towel from her body, letting it fall loosely on the floor around her. "I wanted to wish you a happy birthday," he whispered in her ear. Hannah could smell the beer on his breath; the smell mixing with the steam from the shower, making her feel light-headed.

Hannah stood still, waiting for Jack to make his move. He placed his hands on her shoulders and slowly pushed her down to her knees. He bent down a little and pulled Hannah's head towards him, gently pushing his penis into her mouth. Hannah closed her eyes as he began gyrating back and forth. There were several times when she almost gagged from the force of the attack. When he finished, he zipped his pants up and turned toward the door, staggering a little bit from the lingering effects of the alcohol.

Hannah watched as Jack left the bathroom. Almost robotically, she leaned over the toilet and put her hands down her throat, forcing the vomit to come. She reached into her bag and pulled out her toothbrush and toothpaste, moving the bristles around so hard in her mouth blood started to fall into the sink. She slipped a little as she stepped into the shower, her body slightly trembling. She stood there as the hot water trickled over her, washing away the iniquity down the drain. Grabbing the bar of soap already in the shower, she began rubbing it all over her body, erratically pumping the bar up and down, working hard to remove the dirt. Without thinking, she opened her mouth and moved the bar of soap back and forth across her tongue; the tears flowing down her face as she gagged on the suds. She dropped the bar and watched as it slid down towards the drain. Hannah reached a hand down and turned off the water. She could hear the steady buzz of the bathroom fan, working to eliminate the steam that filled the small bathroom like a heavy fog.

She stepped out of the shower and quickly dressed, leaving her makeup untouched in her bag. Opening the bathroom door, she straightened her shoulders and exhaled as the steam floated out the door. Her Aunt and Uncle would be waiting for her to open her presents, and she was not going to let her stepfather ruin this one last part of her birthday.

Angela Hood & Daphne Cayo

CHAPTER 14

"That's a triple word score," Rose said to her daughters, "which makes it 79 points." She reached towards the bag nonchalantly and started pulling out her replacement letters. Her daughters watched as the smile slowly crept onto her face.

Ellen threw the scorekeeper's pad on the table. "Darn it, Mom!" she said. "That's it, I give up. How am I supposed to catch up with you when you are 150 points ahead? I know why you want to play Scrabble. It just feels too good to beat your children!"

Rose smiled at her daughter. "First of all," she said sweetly, "watch your language. And second of all, I can't help it if the public school system has failed you so terribly… "

Ellen interrupted her mother. "Here we go with the public school system again," she clearing the cups from the table. "And you," she said, looking at Elizabeth. "Are you just going to sit there and say nothing while our mother, our own flesh and blood, creams us over and over again?"

Elizabeth laughed. "She may be sick, but she sure can play Scrabble," she said and leaned over to kiss her mother's cheek. She followed Ellen into the kitchen, bringing the bowl of popcorn kernels. Reaching into the cabinet, she pulled out her mother's pillbox and began emptying the Friday contents into her palm. "Thanks for coming home for the weekend," she said to her sister. Without thinking, Ellen reached a hand down and rubbed her pregnant belly. She was almost five months along now. Using her left foot, she rubbed her right foot, beginning to feel the swell from the day's traveling to make it back home.

"What did the doctor say this week?" she asked Elizabeth. Elizabeth reached a hand to her eyes and wiped away a tear. Before she could even answer, Ellen broke in. "God, Elizabeth," she said, "if you can't handle this, then let me know. You promised me you could take care of Mom until she got better."

"I'm fine, Ellen," she said and straightened up. "The doctor said she's doing better. It's just a bout of the flu, but it shouldn't affect the next round of treatment. If the cancer doesn't come back, they'll label her in remission and things should be fine for a while." The two girls stared down at the floor, both of them thinking the same thing. It was Ellen who finally spoke up and changed the subject.

"What are you going to do about school?"

"Nothing," Elizabeth said staunchly. "I've already decided. I'll be here with Mom as long as she needs me." Ellen didn't say anything and didn't need to. There was no expectation for her to stay with their mother, especially not with the baby coming. Between the child and college, she would have enough to worry about. "And you don't need to worry, Ellen. We're okay. We're doing fine, and Mom is just glad you were able to stay in school." She nodded toward Ellen's stomach, "And she can't wait to meet her first grandchild!" she said, trying her best to sound optimistic.

"Ellen?"

Ellen sat up straight and looked over. She had been lost in a memory of her mother, her mind wandering from the strain of double shifts, Hannah's recent ill temper, and her newest baby girl, Ivy. "Hey, Charlene," she said, "What's up?"

"The patient in 402 is calling for you. He said he only wants you to check his temperature." Charlene rolled her eyes. "You feeling okay? You were just staring off into space."

Ellen stood up and steadied herself on the chair, feeling light-headed. "Of course, I'm fine. It's just the baby, I guess," she said rubbing her stomach. "I'm not as young as I used to be."

Charlene handed her a chart. "Tell Jack to lay off," she said. "You already have two at home. Do you really need another one?" Ellen grabbed the chart and laughed lifting her right foot to rub her left. Her ankles were swelling so badly tonight.

"Speaking of which," she said, "I need to call Hannah and see how Ivy is doing. She hasn't been sleeping so great lately," she said, looking down at the picture of her girls attached to her workstation. Little Ivy was eighteen months old in the picture; her older sister Hannah lovingly cradling her baby sister in her lap. They both looked at the camera at the perfect moment to get the picture. Both her daughters had her mother's smile. Reaching out a finger, she stroked her daughters' faces as she thumbed through the chart. "I'll go to 402," she said, "and take the man's temperature. I swear Mr. Sawyer must have a thing for pregnant women."

Charlene turned to go away. "Make sure you drink water," she told her friend. "It's hot up here tonight." Ellen turned around and headed towards room 402, stopping at the kitchen to pour a cup of water. She could see room 402 from where she was standing and saw the old man sitting on the side of his bed, staring out the window at the abysmal view from his hospital bed. *He's losing weight,* she thought, staring at his frail back. She could see his spine poking out from his dying flesh. She walked into the room and laid a hand on the old man's shoulder. He jumped a little, startled by her presence. "Sorry, Mr. Sawyer," she said. "I'm here to check your temperature."

He nodded and she pulled the machine over popping on the protective tube. "You know the drill," she said reaching towards his mouth.

"Did I ever tell you I was a circus performer in my youth?" he whispered, still staring out the window.

"No, Mr. Sawyer, you didn't," she said, feeling slightly impatient. She wasn't sure if it was the pregnancy, the heat, or a combination of both, but she was starting to get a headache. "What did you do in the circus?"

He looked away from the window and stared at her. "I ate fire, Ellen," he said. "I was a fire-breather. Do you think that's where the cancer came from?"

Ellen leaned against the machine with her free arm. "No, I don't. You have cancer because you smoked like a chimney for most of your life," she said. "Now, come on and let me take your temperature." He opened his mouth *69* like a docile puppy and she put the thermometer in. "You know I'm not even your nurse tonight, right? Charlene's a good nurse. She would love to come in here every two hours and take your temperature." The machine beeped and she pulled out the thermometer.

"I don't want Charlene," he said. "I want you." Ellen sighed and rolled the machine back into the corner.

"You need anything?" she asked.

"When is the baby due?" he said. Ellen stopped and stared at the old man.

"How did you… I mean, did Charlene say something?" she asked.

He swung his legs over the bed and pulled the covers over his atrophied limbs. "My wife and I had seven children. I guess I just know. So, when's the baby due?"

"In about seven months. I just found out a few weeks ago," she said, turning towards the door. "Page me if you need anything, Mr. Sawyer."

"Ellen?" he said. She stopped again, this time making her sigh loud enough for him to hear. "You seem like you're a good mom," he said and dozed off.

Ellen couldn't help but wince when he said it. She had had Hannah out of wedlock, and when she found out she was pregnant with Ivy two years ago, it was on the brink of her marriage falling apart. Ivy had changed things. She just couldn't leave Jack when another one was on the way, and now a third. If she thought too hard about it, she would go crazy. She picked up the phone and dialed the apartment.

"Hello?"

"Hey, sugar," she said to Hannah. "Did Ivy go down alright?"

"Yeah," said Hannah, "she's fine. She cried a little, but then she must have collapsed. She needs a bed, not a crib," the teenager told her mother.

Ellen took a drink of water. "What are you doing tonight?"

"I have a date with Morris," she said. "As soon as Jack comes home from work I'm going to give him a call."

Ellen looked down at another picture on her desk of Hannah. It was the day of her twelfth birthday, standing at her aunt's house in a bright pink swimming suit, a smile as big as the world. It was hard to believe her baby girl was already fifteen and dating boys. It all seemed to be going too fast. "I'll see you tomorrow," she said.

"Bye, Mom," Hannah said. Clicking off her cell phone, Hannah walked into the bathroom and looked in the mirror. She pulled out her eyeliner and touched up her makeup a little fluffing her hair, and straightening her shirt, thinking of her date with Morris.

"Hannah?" she heard Jack call from the front door. *I swear, if he tries anything tonight,* she said to herself. Hannah walked into the hallway and met her stepfather in the front room. He eyed her up and down before he took off his coat. "Going somewhere?"

Hannah nodded. "I'm going out with Morris," she said, pulling out her cell phone. "Ivy's asleep in the bedroom."

Jack walked over and grabbed her cell phone, "Who's Morris?" he asked, smelling her perfume.

"A boy from school," Hannah said, reaching for her phone. "We're just friends."

"If he's just a friend then why all the makeup?" Jack asked, smudging her eyeliner with his thumb. He leaned in and kissed Hannah on the mouth, pulling back as she tightened her lips closed. "You go out too much and with too many different boys."

"Why the hell do you care?" asked Hannah. "Besides, I'm bored."

Jack put his right arm around Hannah's waist and pulled her closer. "We don't have to be bored," said Jack and reached his left hand down to unbutton his pants, "How about let's have some fun, baby? Daddy had a long shift." Hannah pushed him away, hard, and he fell back, tripping over the coffee table.

"It's getting old, Jack," she said roughly. "And I'm not a baby anymore." Jack leapt up from the floor and grabbed her from behind as she turned towards the door to leave.

"Who do you think you are?" he screamed at her. "You think you have a choice?" he screamed and pushed her against the living room wall. Without thinking, Hannah spit in her stepfather's face and tried to knee him in the groin, but he was too fast for her. Using his legs, he forced her legs apart, holding her hands above her head with his left arm as his right unbuttoned his jeans. He flung her onto the carpet and quickly straddled her, pulling her dress over her head and ripping her underwear off. Hannah started screaming, and Jack covered her mouth with his hands as he let the full weight of his body pin her to the floor. Hannah's muffled shrieks filled the apartment as her stepfather forced his way into her, rocking back and forth on top of his stepdaughter. Hannah's legs were writhing on the carpet floor, the young girl struggling with all her might as her stepfather gave a sudden jerk of movement and collapsed on top of her, wiping the sweat from his forehead with her soiled dress.

Jack stood up and buckled his pants once again. He threw Hannah's dress onto her stomach. "Was that fun for you?" he asked. He leaned down over his stepdaughter once more and pulled her limp body off the carpet. Silent tears were streaming down Hannah's face. He kissed her, forcing his tongue into her mouth, licking her upper and lower gums as if he were a wild animal, enjoying the last savory bites of the kill. He dropped his stepdaughter onto the carpet. "Put your clothes on before your mom gets home," he ordered. Hannah lay motionless until she heard his bedroom door swing shut.

Silently, she gathered her dress and her ripped underwear off the floor. She walked to her bedroom door and slowly turned the handle, trying hard not to wake Ivy. The little girl lay in her crib, curled in a tight ball, hugging her teddy bear. Slowly, Hannah opened her dresser drawer and pulled out a new pair of underwear. Next, she went to the closet and chose another dress, leaving the closet light on so she could see her way to bed when she returned. Closing the door softly, Hannah walked into the bathroom and looked in the mirror. Like a robot, she took her eyeliner out of her purse straightening her makeup; licking a tissue to wipe off the smudges. Once she slipped her dress over her head and pulled her new underwear on, she pulled out her cell phone and stared at the keypad. The tears kept streaming down her face and, as hard as she tried, Hannah couldn't stop them. Her hand was shaking as she pushed the call button. "I'm ready," she said into the phone. "I'll be waiting outside."

Hannah opened the apartment door and stepped out into the humid July
night. As she walked into the parking lot, she threw her underwear and

dress from before into the dumpster and looked back at the apartment window. "I hate you," she whispered and turned towards the approaching headlights.

"I hate you."

"I hate you."

Angela Hood *&* Daphne Cayo

CHAPTER 15

Elizabeth reached into the cabinet and pulled out the garlic powder. Flipping the top, she sprinkled the spice haphazardly over the stir-fry sizzling in the pan. She placed the garlic powder on the counter and once again stared at the purple and white stick lying on the paper towel. The single line was all she needed to know: a single line dashing any hope that she and Connor would ever conceive.

"Why do you keep doing this, Liz?" asked Connor, picking up the pregnancy test and tossing it into the trash can. "It's torture, honey, it's masochistic." He put his arms around her shoulders and kissed the back of her head.

"I know you're right," she said, staring down into the cooking vegetables. She couldn't bear to look at his face. "I know it's silly to keep buying tests and peeing on little sticks. I just…" before she could stop herself she began sobbing, reaching up with her hands to grip Connor's forearms that had tightened around her. "It's just so unfair. We would love a child so much. Why wouldn't God…"

Connor interrupted her. "Hush, Lizzie. Don't blame God for this, honey. If He's keeping a child from us, there must be a reason. Come on," he said, reaching down and turning off the fire. "Let's sit down to dinner and then go out. We can go shopping, go watch a movie, whatever you want… your pick." She smiled at her husband and walked over to the rice cooker the smell of jasmine rice filling the kitchen. *Just like a man,* she thought, Connor trying his hardest to fix everything when she wasn't asking him to fix it.

I actually just feel like staying in tonight, Connor. Thanks for the offer, it's really sweet, but I would love to just put on some sweatpants and curl up in front of the TV." They set the table in silence and Connor turned on some jazz music to fill the awkward silence of the evening. She watched with her eyes open as Connor bowed his head and said grace over the meal. She sipped the red wine, letting the soothing heat flow through her the warm liquid calming her anxiety. "Okay, I promise you no more tests."

He smiled. "No more tests? You promise. Pinky swear?" he said, holding out his little finger. She laughed and wrapped her finger around his. Using the strength of his finger, he pulled her close and gently kissed her. "You're never going to believe what a client requested today for their reception."

"I can only imagine."

"A petting zoo," replied Connor

Elizabeth choked on her wine.

"Excuse me? A petting zoo at a wedding?" she laughed.

"That's right. Apparently, the bride and groom met at a petting zoo where they both brought their kids. They are both divorced, of course, and the rest is history. I guess the smell of manure wafting in from the camel ride is what sealed the deal!"

"Honestly, Connor," she said, "What did you tell them?"

The phone rang and Connor rose from the table. Hello?" he said into the receiver. There was silence on the other end. "Hello?"

"Uncle Connor?" a timid voice was heard through the phone.

"Hannah?" he said. Elizabeth turned around quickly in her chair. *What's wrong?* she mouthed to Connor. He shrugged his shoulders. "Hannah, are you alright?"

There was another hesitation on the end of the line. "Can I talk to Aunt Liz, please?" she asked. Connor could tell she was on the brink of tears.

"Sure, of course, honey." He handed the phone to Elizabeth, who had already risen from her seat and was motioning for the receiver.

"Hannah, its Aunt Liz. What's wrong? Where are you? Do you need help? Are you okay?" The words came spilling out; filling the awkward silence before Hannah could even respond.

"I'm fine, Aunt Liz," she said, trying to convince herself. "I was just won dering, I mean, if you aren't doing anything, could you come and pick me up?"

"Pick you up?" said Elizabeth. "From where? Where are you, Hannah?" There was a long pause on the other end of the phone, and Elizabeth could hear Hannah trying to hold back sobs.

"I'm at the police station," she said so quietly her aunt could barely hear her. Elizabeth sighed and leaned against the counter.

"Hannah, what happened?" her tone had changed.

"I got caught shoplifting," she told her aunt. "I was with some friends, and Morris said he does it all the time, so I thought, no big deal… "

This time it was Elizabeth who interrupted her niece. "I'm not really interested in the story, Hannah," she said. "Have you called your mother?"

"No, I was thinking maybe you could come and get me, and I could stay with you for a while or something."

"Hannah, you know I love you, but you need to call your mother. You can't come and hide out here. If you don't call your mother, I will." She waited for her niece to respond but was met with silence once again. "Hannah, are you going to call… "She stopped as the line went dead. Hannah had hung up the phone. Lizzie hung up the phone and set it back on the counter.

"Well?" asked Connor. "What was that about?"

Elizabeth sat down and poured another glass of wine. "She was shoplifting and got caught. She's at the police station."

"Hannah? That doesn't seem like her. I know she's getting older, but our Hannah wouldn't do something like that. It must be a misunderstanding."

"What should I do? Should I call Ellen or give Hannah time to do it? I just don't know what's going on with her, Connor. She's more like her mother every day. I can remember when Ellen was Hannah's age. She was bound and determined to get in trouble, like she sought it out."

"Hannah's not Ellen," replied Connor. "I think you should call your sister. Hannah's still just a kid, Lizzie, and if she doesn't call Ellen she'll spend the night at the police station." He handed her the phone.

Elizabeth dialed her sister's number, dreading the impending conversation. *77*

Ellen picked up, sounding groggy. "Ellen? Did I wake you up?" Elizabeth glanced at the clock. It was only seven thirty in the evening.

Ellen yawned. "Yeah, I was just taking a nap. Too many night shifts at the hospital, I guess. What's up?"

Elizabeth glanced at Connor, who took the cue and left the kitchen with his dinner plate. She could hear the TV in the living room click on. "I just got a call from Hannah, and she's at the police station. She was picked up for shoplifting. She asked me to come and get her, but I told her I would call you." She said it quickly and waited for her sister to respond. Just like Hannah, Ellen sat on the other end of the phone not saying a word. "Ellen?"

"Thanks for calling me," Ellen said curtly. "I'll let you know if we need anything else. Good night, Lizzie." The phone clicked off, and Elizabeth sighed once again. She looked down at her cold stir-fry and decided to join Connor in the living room.

"Something's wrong, Connor," she said. "I can't pinpoint it yet, but something's not right."

❧

Ellen lay panting in the backseat, squished under the weight of the boy on top of her. His hands were all over her and the heat inside had steamed up the windows; creating a façade of privacy for the young couple against the cold air outside the car. She leaned her head backwards, arching her back as he kissed her neck. "Come on, Gary," she breathed, "I'm already late and I need to get inside." The young boy pulled her closer, running his fingers through her hair.

"Just a few more minutes, baby," he whispered in her ear. "Ain't you cozy in here, too?" He smiled down at her. She was becoming uncomfortable with his full weight pushing against her stomach. She pushed herself up on her elbows and kissed him on the cheek.

"You're squashing me," she said, and he backed off. "If I hurry in, hopefully she'll still be asleep." She glanced at the radio and saw the time: 3:30 am. "Gary," she screamed, this time pushing the young boy off her. "It's after three in the morning!" She brushed the beer bottle off her coat, grabbed her purse, opened the backseat door, and ran across the yard to the door.

The snow crunched under her feet and she stumbled a little on the ice covering the bottom step. She tried to get her balance, but fell, hitting her shin on the step. "Ow!" she mumbled and sat down, rubbing her leg with her nearly frozen hand. A cold, wet liquid was spreading across her jeans and she jumped up, looking down at the pile of melted snow that had formed around the snow salt. "Great," she muttered and brushed the snow off her pants. She fumbled in her purse for the keys and remembered she placed them in her backpack that morning. She must have forgotten to transfer them to her purse before she left with Gary. Turning the knob, she hoped for a miracle, and it swung open into the front parlor. "Thank, God," she whispered and stepped inside.

"I wouldn't bring God into this," her mother said. Ellen jumped, startled to hear her mother.

"Geez, Mom," she said. "I didn't see you there. You scared the crap out of me," she said, laughing nervously. She looked over at her mother, who was sitting in the front room a small table lamp aglow beside her. Ellen saw right away that from her seat she had had a perfect view of Gary's car. "I can explain, Mom," said Ellen. Rose lifted a hand to her daughter and got up from her chair.

Without saying a word, she walked toward the staircase and put her hand on the banister. Ellen stood in the front room, wishing her mother would say something… anything. She couldn't bear the silence as her mother abruptly turned away and began walking upstairs.

Rose hesitated on the second step of the landing and turned around to face her daughter. "You're beautiful, Ellen," Rose said suddenly. "And there are a lot of guys who will want that beauty. They look at you and they think how amazing it would be to have just a little bit of you. They think if they can just take a piece of you they'll feel so good about themselves." She stopped and examined her daughter, who had taken a seat in the armchair Rose had just occupied. "I know you never really had a daddy, Ellen, and if I could turn time back…" Rose's voice trailed off. She looked at her daughter, who looked so young in the dim light of the winter's evening. There was so much she wanted to say to her daughter and so much, she knew Ellen wouldn't really understand. "Do you love this Gary?" she finally asked her daughter.

Ellen shrugged her shoulders. "I don't know. He's funny. He holds my *79* hand at school and it makes me feel not so alone, I guess," she said. It had been a while since she'd talked to her mother about anything, let alone her boyfriend.

Rose opened her mouth, trying to figure out what to say, faltering as the words came out so clumsily. "Please be careful, Ellen," she finally managed. "Don't cheapen your life." She walked back down the steps toward her daughter and kissed her on the cheek. "And by the way, you can shovel the driveway tomorrow morning. Seven a.m. sharp." Ellen nodded as her mother turned off the light. "Time for bed." Rose led her daughter up the stairs and watched as she turned the bathroom light on and closed the door.

Sometimes it was too much. She knew shoveling the driveway was a pitiful punishment for missing curfew by three and a half hours. Perhaps she hoped the sweat that fell from her daughter as she worked would somehow cleanse her of any sins committed the night before. Half the time, she didn't know what she was doing and, just like her daughter, felt alone. The shower water came on in the bathroom and Rose walked into her own room. Pulling the covers up and over, she slowly fell asleep, catching what little darkness was left in the night.

Ellen sat on the cold, plastic chair in the police station and watched as her daughter was ushered into the waiting room. Hannah approached her mother and stared at her, eye-to-eye, almost as if she were daring her mother to look away first. Ellen didn't remove her gaze from her daughter. "Thank you, officer," she said and turned toward the front door, herself daring her daughter to follow.

She stepped into the car, slamming the door. Hannah opted for the back seat, slamming the door behind her as well. "A little humility would be appreciated, you know," Ellen said to her daughter, who had slumped down in the backseat. She noticed that Hannah's thick black eyeliner was smudged on the right side. It looked like she had been crying and hastily fixed herself.

"Whatever," Hannah said pulling out her iPod. Closing her eyes, she tried to fill her brain with the music, but it didn't work. She realized how lucky she had been, getting off with a warning. All she had to do was pay the store back for the merchandise.

Ellen turned the car radio on and fastened her safety belt moving it down over her pregnant belly. She was beginning to show and the seatbelt felt tight. She reached down and scratched her stomach before putting the car in drive and pulling out of the precinct parking lot.

The ride home was filled with awkward silence, the DJ filling the void with hip-hop music that seemed too upbeat for the mood in the car. The apartment parking lot had filled while Ellen was picking up her daughter, and she had to park farther away than usual from their building. She and Hannah walked to the door, side by side in total silence, as Ellen struggled with what to say. On one hand, she wanted to slap her daughter's face and yell at her to wake up. Didn't she see the path she was taking, heading in the same direction as Ellen herself had? But on the other hand, she wanted to hold her daughter tight and never let go. She thought of her mother and felt the tears slowly forming in her eyes. It had been so long since she had thought of Rose.

They entered the front door of the apartment and Jack looked up from the couch. He had dozed off; a sleeping Ivy curled up on the couch beside him. Hannah looked at him, looked at her mother, and lost it. "I hate this house and everyone in it!" she screamed, running to her room and slamming the door shut behind her.

"Hannah!" Ellen screamed and ran to her daughter's door as the lock button clicked on the other side. "Hannah! Young lady, open this door right now! "She said to the wood frame. She fiddled with the knob once more and listened to the silence coming from the other side. She couldn't stop the tears forming in her eyes as she walked into the bedroom and fell, exhausted, onto the bed. She felt a small kick inside of her and placed her hand on her stomach; slowly rubbing the stretched skin as more tears fell on her pillow.

Angela Hood & Daphne Cayo

CHAPTER 16

It was a warm day for December and the sun was shining, glaring off the leftover snow mounds in the front yard. Elizabeth looked down from her bedroom window at the now-covered pool in the backyard. It already seemed like this year's winter in Chicago was never going to end, and it had only just begun. Going back to the hall closet, she began removing the tubs marked "Christmas." She realized she had much more stuff than she had originally thought and began thinking about where all of the garlands, wreaths, and trees would go around the house. Christmas was always her mother's favorite holiday, and she had passed on the bug to her daughter.

"Honey!" Connor called from the front room. "Your sister's on the line!" Lizzie leaned her head out of the closet and pulled a cobweb from her arm. She had been so engrossed in the process she hadn't even heard the phone ring.

"Coming," she yelled down to Connor, pulling the last remnants of the web off her sweater. "Ellen?" she spoke into the receiver. "I was just thinking of you and all the Christmases with Mom. I was just getting ready to pull down the old ornament box. You and the girls should come over soon," she said. "And of course, Jack, too." Elizabeth was smiling, her festive spirit growing as she heard Christmas music playing from the stereo downstairs. *Knowing Connor, he had probably heated up hot chocolate on the stove,* she thought. "Ellen?" she asked, thinking her sister's cell phone battery might have died when her sister didn't respond.

"I'm here," Ellen said. "I have a favor to ask of you, Lizzie. I was wondering if you could take Hannah for a while until Jack and I figure out what to do about her."

Elizabeth sighed and switched the phone to her other ear. "What's been going on?" she asked.

"She's just out of control, and Jack and the doctor think I need a calmer environment. I only have another month before the baby's due, and if I didn't have, Hannah to worry about I think it might go more smoothly. It would only be for a month."

"What does Hannah think?" asked Elizabeth. She leaned over the upstairs banister and looked down into the living room. Sure enough, Connor was sitting on the couch, sipping a cup of hot cocoa, staring into the fire.

"She's okay with it," said Ellen. "I think she needs a break from me as much as I need one from her."

"I can ask Connor to come by tonight and pick her up," she said. "I have an office holiday planning meeting I have to be at, but I won't be home late."

"Thank you, Elizabeth."

Elizabeth could tell her sister was straining to say the words. She couldn't remember the last time Ellen had thanked her for anything. "Don't worry about it. We're family." She clicked the phone off and headed downstairs to Connor.

"Everything okay?" he asked. She knew by now her husband was suspicious whenever her sister called. It was usually because she needed something.

"I think Hannah's going to stay with us for a while," she said, looking at him out the corner of her eye. He raised his cocoa to his lips and took a long sip. The warm liquid took away the chill he had from scraping the last few chunks of ice from the front steps.

"I think that's a great idea," he said, smiling at his wife. "Do you want me to pick her up tonight?"

"Whenever you're ready. I leave for my work thing in an hour, or else I would do it myself. I'll get the guest room ready." She stood up from the couch and Connor grabbed her wrist, pulling her back down.

"I know why we have to do this," he said. "I just want to make sure you're ready for it. Work is really stressful for you right now, and I know your promotion is on the line. If it's too much, you can always tell your sister you've changed your mind."

Elizabeth reached over and kissed him on the cheek. It was so like him to worry about her, putting her feelings in front of any inconveniences the situation might bring about for him. "I feel like I don't have a choice, actually. I was just going through the Christmas stuff and found the box of old ornaments that I kept from Mom's house. I remember my first Christmas without her, stuck in that crummy little apartment with the tree I found in the thrift store. Mom always loved Christmas so much. She said it was the one time of year when you felt like you could start over. 'Christmas is my New Year's,' she would say. Maybe it can be the same for Hannah."

Connor reached up and lovingly stroked his wife's hair. She was aging so beautifully; each year making her more and more lovely. He remembered the frightened young woman he had approached at that wedding so many years ago. He'd seen a light in his wife from across the room and was captivated at first glance. She seemed so out of place at the gathering; those big eyes staring around, looking for a place to hide. He had no idea he would be this happy with her. "I love you," he said looking deeply into her eyes.

"I love you, too," Elizabeth replied. She stood up and headed towards the guest room, tidying up a few things before Hannah arrived that evening.

From across the room, Hannah started throwing her clothes into the suitcase, intentionally creating a mess for her mother to clean up after she left. They had moved into a bigger apartment weeks ago, one with a third bedroom for Ivy and the new baby. Even though Hannah had a room to herself, she felt less comfortable. Ever since Ivy was born, Jack had relaxed on Hannah. There had been no more late night rendezvous in her bedroom while his little daughter lay asleep in a crib not five feet from Hannah's bed. Then her mom started working the late shift again, and all hell broke loose in the young girl's life.

She was mad at her mother; mad she didn't notice Hannah's cries for help. How much louder did she need to be for her mother to listen to her, to notice her amidst the swarm of babies being brought into the house? As much as Hannah loved Ivy, it sickened her to think of her stepfather making love to her mother, all the while plotting his next encounter with her. The guilt was overwhelming when she thought about how little she anticipated the new baby as well.

In all honesty, the move to her aunt's house should have brought great relief to the young girl. It was a chance to get away from Jack and feel safe again. But the truth was, Hannah didn't feel safe anywhere. She spent more and more time away from the apartment, finding solace in the arms of her boyfriend. To her, the sex she had to give him was a fair trade for a place to be that was far away from her stepfather.

The bag was filled to capacity now. There was no more room for any of her belongings, and now she looked around at the scattered items on the floor. She realized she probably should clean them up, but decided to leave them on the floor. More than likely, when she came back home, they would still be sitting on the floor of her room. Quickly, she threw her makeup into her purse and headed out into the living room. Her mother and Jack were sitting at the dining room table holding hands. When Hannah came into the room, Jack pulled his hand away and stared at his stepdaughter.

"All packed?" asked her mother, trying desperately to ease the tension.

"Sure," Hannah said, lugging her suitcase to the front door.

"It's only for a few weeks, okay?" said Ellen. "Until the baby is born and things get settled. We just need some air, you know?"

"Sure," she said again, "I get it." Ellen jumped as the buzzer sounded and realized Connor was standing on the landing downstairs. She watched as her daughter opened the door and left, not bothering to say goodbye. As Hannah closed the door, she caught her stepfather's eyes and glared fiercely into his face. *You can end it all here,* she said to herself. *You can let your mother know what that jerk has done to you.* The moment was gone as the door slammed shut. Inside the apartment, Ellen collapsed face down on the table; the tears pouring into the already stained oak varnish. Jack put a hand on her shoulder and stared down at his wife.

By force of habit, Hannah sat in the back seat of her Uncle's car. "I feel like a chauffeur," he joked as he turned the keys. "Where to, madam?" He looked at Hannah in the rear view mirror. She tried to smile but for the first time felt the stinging sensation of tears. From Connor's view, Hannah looked like a frightened animal; like a baby bunny whose nest had been discovered by a predator, the way she cowered in the backseat. They drove to the house in silence.

Connor unlocked the front door and opened it for Hannah. Still clutching her suitcase and purse, Hannah walked into the familiar house, feeling for the first time like an unwanted annoyance rather than an invited guest. Her uncle locked the doors behind her and Hannah jumped, turning around quickly to look at her uncle. He reached out to take her bags and Hannah jerked them away. "Where's Aunt Liz?" she asked, not hiding the anxiousness in her voice. She noticed the hurt look in her uncle's eyes at being met with such suspicion.

Connor took a step away from the young girl and turned on the porch light as well as the lights to the living room. "She had a work meeting," he said, backing away a little more. "I'm sorry," he said to Hannah, "I should have asked you first. Do you mind if I carry your bags to your room?"

"No, that's okay," Hannah, said. "I mean, thanks for the offer, but I can get it myself. It's just that they aren't that heavy."

Connor backed up even more. "Have you had dinner? I think there are leftovers in the fridge. Or I can heat you up some hot chocolate. I think other than that, all we have is diet soda and water. I'll have to go to the store tomorrow and pick up some snacks." He looked at his niece, trying hard to hide the worry plastered on his face. "Your room is the downstairs guest room, just down the hall. The one with the bathroom attached. Make yourself at home, Hannah. You are welcome for as long as you need to be here."

Hannah nodded at Connor and walked into the bedroom. She noticed her aunt had framed a picture of the two of them from the last barbeque and placed it on the dresser. Stuck to the picture frame was a note that said "Welcome!" in her aunt's beautiful handwriting. Hannah turned on the light and looked around. She sat on the bed, and the plush comforter sunk around her. Aunt Lizzie had even laid out towels for her on the bed and placed small samples of shampoo, conditioner and body wash on top of the washcloth.

Hannah locked her bedroom door and took out a change of clothes. Walking into the bathroom, she turned on the shower and looked in the mirror. Her heavy eyeliner made her eyes appear smaller, almost sunken, as the grey eye shadow created a tough girl illusion on her porcelain skin. Steam started filling the room as Hannah stepped into the shower, once again letting the hot water roll over her. She wasn't sure how long she stayed in the shower, but it felt like days. A part of her wanted to hide amidst the wall of water droplets until she felt things getting better. She looked down at her hands and saw her fingers starting to wrinkle. Turning off the water, she reached for her towel and stepped onto the bathroom rug. Even the rugs in her aunt's house felt expensive. Her feet sunk into the fibers, which felt as soft as silk underneath her feet.

She didn't intend to fall asleep before her aunt came home, but as soon as her head hit the pillow, she was out. Whether or not the young girl realized it, she desperately needed a good night's sleep. For the first time in a long time, she slept without fear.

CHAPTER 17

The red, green, and white decorations at the mall made even the most cynical shopper a little more cheerful. Elizabeth couldn't help but smile as the Christmas music played overhead; barely heard above the chatter of the shoppers, crammed shoulder-to-shoulder in the packed shopping center, picking up the final few things for Christmas. She couldn't believe the holiday was only two weeks away. She looked over at her niece who was staring down at the floor; hardly lifting her feet during the celebration around her. "Come on, Hannah," said Lizzie. "Cheer up. What if I bought you an early Christmas present today?" Hannah smiled at her niece affectionately.

"That's okay, Aunt Lizzie. I'd feel bad taking anything else from you."

"Well, at least enjoy the music and the fake Santas," said Elizabeth. "You're never too old to believe in Santa, right? Oh, look!" she yelled suddenly and pulled Hannah over to one of the many store windows. "I've been looking for a tie like this for months for Connor. Your uncle, Hannah, may be a wonderful man, but he's a lousy dresser! Have you seen his wardrobe recently and that God-awful purple tie he keeps wearing? Come on," she said as she led Hannah inside the store. The young girl stood by the opening of the door, watching as the sales woman helped her aunt and boxed up the tie. Ever since her aunt married Connor, she had been so happy. Living with them this week, Hannah couldn't help but wonder what her life would be like if she had been born to her aunt and Connor. Each day that went by brought a pang of sadness to Hannah because it meant one day closer to returning to the apartment and the heavy hands of her stepfather.

"Ready?" asked Elizabeth. Hannah looked at her aunt and nodded. She stopped short when her cell phone started ringing; synchronized perfectly with the security posts on either side of the exit, her cell phone set off the security bell. Before they knew it, a security guard walked to the front of the store.

"Can I see your receipt, ma'am?" he asked. Elizabeth looked confused and showed him her receipt.

"I'm sorry, officer," she said to the man. "We were just leaving when my niece's cell phone went off. It must have triggered the alarm."

"Harold." The sales lady who had just helped her aunt came rushing over. "I just checked her out. She's fine."

He looked over the receipt and handed it back. "Not a problem. Sorry for the inconvenience. It's just that we always have a spike in shoplifters around this time of year. I just need to check the young girl's purse, too, just to be sure." Hannah stood frozen and pulled her purse to her chest.

"What do you mean, 'check my purse'?" she asked the officer. "I wasn't doing anything wrong. My aunt told you, my cell phone went off and triggered it."

Elizabeth laughed nervously and nudged her niece. "Just let him look through your purse, Hannah. It's fine. Let the man do his job."

"No," said Hannah resolutely. "I don't see how his job is to *assume* I've shoplifted. Besides," she said hotly, "my mom always, says when you assume it makes a fool out of you, and… "

"Hannah!" her aunt interrupted with a horrified look on her face. "Apologize! What's gotten into you? Just let him look through your purse so we can go." Hannah stared at the security guard. She could tell he was trying to keep his cool. Between his reddening face and the disappointed gaze her aunt was giving her, Hannah wished she hadn't started any of it. Honestly, she didn't know why it happened at all, and the small crowd forming around them didn't help. She noticed one young girl had even taken her cell phone out and was snapping a picture. Rolling her eyes, she tossed the bag at the guard, her purse strap knocking him in the nose. He leafed through the purse and then handed it back to Hannah.

"Happy holidays," he muttered sarcastically and turned away.

Elizabeth pulled Hannah out of the store and into a hallway lined with lockers and signs pointing to the restroom. "Hannah, what on earth was that?" she asked her niece, her arms folded as she looked into her eyes. "Well?" At the worst moment possible, the tune of "Jingle Bells" started playing from Elizabeth's purse. She hesitated at first, then reached in and grabbed her cell phone. "Hello? Oh, hi, Jack," she said, still looking at Hannah. She noticed the young girl flinch when she said her stepfather's name. "Oh, my, it's early, but it's wonderful news. Yes, of course I'll tell Hannah. And, Jack? Congratulations!"

"It's the baby, isn't it?" said Hannah.

"Yes, honey," Elizabeth, said, her tone softening. "You have a baby brother, Tyson Jack. He was born about an hour ago." Hannah could tell her aunt was trying to sound happy about the baby, but she still looked worried, her face showing confusion over what had happened. "Hannah, I didn't think you had taken anything. I don't think just because you've shoplifted before means you're going to do it again." Elizabeth looked at her niece, searching for any sign of understanding on the young girl's face. She could tell Hannah was holding back tears, biting her lower lip in an attempt to keep the drops from falling from her eyes. She reached out and hugged her niece. "I love you, Hannah," she said. "You know that, right?" Hannah nodded and wiped a tear away with the back of her hand. Looking down, she saw a smudge of eyeliner and excused herself to the restroom.

Hannah reached down and activated the motion sensor to turn the faucet water on. It was freezing cold and sprayed a little onto her coat sleeve. A woman and her young daughter came out of the stalls behind her. The mother saw her and quickly ushered her daughter to the next sink, washing hurriedly and wiping her daughter's hands on her jeans. "Mommy, is that the girl who took stuff at the store?" she heard the little girl ask her mother. "Shhh," the mother said hurriedly as they scurried out the door.

Hannah walked into the stall and latched the door closed behind her. She was feeling sick to her stomach, and the walls of the bathroom slowly started spinning. Trying to focus on the sales flyer taped to the stall door, she steadied herself, sliding down the stall to sit on the cold linoleum.

"Hannah?" She saw her aunt's shoes standing outside the stall. "Are you feeling okay?"

"Yeah, I'm fine," she said, getting up. The rush of air that hit her from the heating unit above caused the dizziness to return. Reaching for her aunt, she steadied herself once more. "I just feel funny all of a sudden."

Elizabeth looked at her niece and led her out of the bathroom. "Come on," she said. "Let's get some fresh air." A light snow had started falling, making the pavement of the parking lot slightly slippery as they walked towards her aunt's car. Hannah was feeling better as she climbed into the front seat. Christmas music flooded the car as her aunt turned the ignition. She quickly shut off the radio and pulled out of the parking lot. "I talked to your mom while you were in the bathroom. She asked if you could come back home tonight and watch Ivy while she and Tyson spent the night at the hospital. Jack has to work tonight. He couldn't find anyone to take over his shift, so I'll stay at the hospital with your mom and then, after being home for a few days, if you want to come back to our place, that's fine."

"Thanks, Aunt Liz," she said, "but I imagine my mom will need a lot of help with the new baby. I should probably stay at home, if my mom says its okay."

"We'll go home and get your things, then. Do you want to come to the hospital with me and see Tyson or just go straight to the apartment?"

"Just take me home first," she said. "I'm sure I'll see plenty of Tyson later on." Elizabeth couldn't imagine what her niece must be feeling; first Ivy and now Tyson, when Hannah herself was almost seventeen. If she was honest with the situation, she didn't know what her sister was thinking either. She understood Ivy was an accident, but then when Jack pushed for another, the entire thing seemed ridiculous to her. She imagined Hannah must feel left out, especially after being sent to live with her and Connor. Her niece had changed so much in the past four years it was hard to believe she was the same girl who had torn into her birthday presents and raced Connor around the swimming pool. Her eyes seemed distant now; revealing an inner hurt Elizabeth could never get her to talk about. There was a depth of sadness in her niece well beyond her years.

Inside the house, Elizabeth told Connor the news. He walked back to Hannah's room and knocked on the door. She jumped at the sound and took a step back when she saw it was Connor. Seeing her eyes widen when he stepped into the room, he took a step back out. "I was just wondering if you needed help packing," he said. "Or, if you're finished, I can take your bag to the car."

"Oh," she said. "I'm okay. I still have a few things to pack." Her uncle's heart ached as he looked at the young girl. She wore clothes that were too tight and her heavy makeup covered up her beautiful almond eyes. Her foundation was a shade too light for her fair complexion; leaving a pasty glow that hid the perfect skin underneath. He barely recognized her as the same girl who used to shower him with hugs and innocent affection.

As he walked away from her room, he couldn't hold back the tears. More than anything, he wanted to hold her in his arms and tell her everything would be all right, but his presence seemed to bother her more than help. Walking into the kitchen, he saw his wife standing at the back door, looking out over the snowfall in the backyard. He put his arms around her waist and kissed her neck. A few tears fell onto her hair, leaving damp patches.

"You okay?" she asked him, hearing him trying to cover up his emotions.

"I just miss the old Hannah," he said, his voice quivering slightly. "How long are you going to be gone?"

"Just one night, I think. She needs someone there to help with the baby."

"Something's not right, honey," Connor whispered in her ear. "…something about Hannah. My presence makes her so uncomfortable, it's like she's scared of me. Whenever I get near, she cowers like an animal about to be attacked. You don't think something has happened to her, do you?"

Elizabeth turned to look at him. "What do you mean?" she asked, her eyes narrowing. "Like what?"

Connor rubbed his wife's arm. "I don't know. She's been dating a lot of boys lately. Maybe there was something with one of them at school. She's just lost that…" he struggled to find the word, "that innocence, I guess."

Elizabeth sat her coffee mug on the counter. "She is almost seventeen, Connor," she said. "But I do agree she's not the same Hannah. She's had a rough couple of years with Ivy and now Tyson being born. I think it's just that. She's got to feel like the odd man out."

Connor nodded his head, not completely convinced that was the problem. He saw the shadow of Hannah coming down the hallway and met her halfway, gently taking her bag and heading toward the garage. Hannah and Elizabeth followed, Elizabeth holding her own overnight bag. Connor *93* took his wife's bag and threw it in the backseat, gently kissing her as she got into the car. He walked over to Hannah and awkwardly gave her a side hug before heading inside.

Elizabeth tried to chatter and fill the car ride with noise, but the awkward silence coming from her niece drowned out all of her attempts. They pulled up to the apartment building and Hannah reached over to give her aunt a hug that was more out of obligation than desire. Reaching into the backseat for her bag, Hannah accidentally elbowed her aunt on the cheek.

"Oh, God, Aunt Lizzie, I'm so sorry," she said, her face horrified at the accident.

Elizabeth rubbed her cheek and laughed. "Hannah, it was an accident, and it's not a big deal. Your stepfather should be back with Ivy any minute. I'll see you soon." She hugged her niece once again and watched as she stepped out of the car and slowly made her way to the front door, lugging her bag behind her.

Hannah walked into the door of their apartment and headed straight to her bedroom. To her surprise, her mother had cleaned her room during the time she had been gone. The scattered clothes were folded neatly and placed on her bed, and the lemony smell meant someone had dusted recently. She placed her bag on the bed and unzipped the top, taking out the picture of her and Aunt Liz that had been in her bedroom. Staring at the picture, she closed her eyes and tried to imagine herself standing on the back patio, all of those years ago.

"Welcome home," her stepfather said from the door.

"Hannah!" Ivy ran past her father and jumped up onto Hannah's lap. "I missed you!" the young girl said, kissing her sister on the cheek. Hannah hugged the little girl and watched as she skipped out of the room. In a few seconds, Hannah heard the noises of cartoons coming from the TV. Hannah eyed her stepfather as he continued to stare at her.

"I guess you've heard your mother had the baby," he said awkwardly, approaching his stepdaughter. "You know, it's been a long time." Walking closer to Hannah, he swung the door closed behind him and turned the lock.

94   "Jack," Hannah pleaded, "…come on. Ivy's just in the front room."

"No," he reassured her. "It's her favorite show. And besides, I've got needs, too, baby girl." He pushed the freshly folded laundry off her bed, sending it sprawling across the floor. Hannah closed her eyes and fell back, imagining herself asleep on the plush bed at her aunt's house with the door locked safely behind her.

Zipping his pants, her stepfather walked towards the bedroom door. "I'll be gone until tomorrow morning," he said, his voice emotionless as he opened her door and let himself out. Hannah dressed herself and walked into the living room to find Ivy asleep on the couch; the glow of the TV casting shadows on the wall. She lifted the small child and carried her to the crib inside the second bedroom. She was getting too big for the confined space, but she quickly found her favorite corner and rolled up around her teddy bear. Stroking her hair, Hannah stood at the side of the crib for a few minutes. "If he ever touches you," she whispered, "I'll kill him." She thought of Tyson and envied the newborn, envied his gender that would shield him from the many hurts in her own life.

Walking back into her room, she gathered her pajamas from her luggage and stepped into the bathroom. Her mother must have started labor in here because things were scattered, almost as if someone had fallen and knocked the contents of the counter onto the floor. Baby shampoo, a hair comb, and several odds and ends were lying on the floor. Hannah picked them up and tried to remember their placement on the bathroom counter before stepping into the shower and once again letting the steam create a wall between her and the outside world.

Angela Hood & Daphne Cayo

CHAPTER 18

"Is it a boy or a girl?" the saleswoman asked Elizabeth, who was circling the display of baby presents in the hospital gift shop.

"It's a boy. His name is Tyson," she said, "and he's the first boy in the family. Up until now it's been all girls!"

"How exciting!" the woman said, her hands reaching out for several items on the shelf. "Here's a beautiful little blue teddy bear that's been popular, or this cute sleeper with the matching baseball cap. They are both perfect for a newborn."

Elizabeth looked at each of the items, stroking the soft fur of the teddy bear and admiring the stitching on the sleeper, sewed to look like a miniature uniform. "My husband would love this," she told the woman. "He's a baseball fanatic!"

"Oh," the woman brightened. "Do you have children?"

Elizabeth shook her head and turned away; biting her lip to keep back the tears that suddenly sprang into her eyes. "This is my sister's third, though," she said, forcing the humor to come into her voice. "I think she's having enough babies for both of us!" she tried to laugh. The saleswoman didn't notice the small quiver in her voice and gave a slight chuckle.

"Shall I wrap one up for you, then?"

"I'll take both," Elizabeth decided. "And why don't you put them in a gift basket with some stuffing and a card." The woman seemed happy at the suggestion and filled a basket with a few other small goodies she insisted Elizabeth purchase to make it look just right. In the end, Elizabeth was hauling a rather stuffed blue basket with the teddy bear, sleeper, a small copy of *Goodnight Moon*, and some lavender scented lotion for her sister. It was wrapped in cellophane with a small card dangling from the curling ribbon at the top.

Hastily, Elizabeth scrawled the words "Love, Connor and Elizabeth" onto the card before the saleswoman attached it to the basket. She wasn't sure what else to say or how she felt about this new baby at all. She couldn't deny the twinge of jealousy that hit her heart whenever she thought of her sister's ease in conceiving. It seemed like all she and Jack had to do was look at each other and conception began. Their apartment was already bursting at the seams with three. Elizabeth couldn't imagine where little Tyson was going to sleep or how they were going to make ends meet, for that matter. Her sister was already working overtime each week while Jack hopped from job to job, his employment as unsteady as their financial situation.

She walked to her sister's room and gently knocked on the door. Walking, in she found Tyson cradled in Ellen's arm, sucking on a bottle of formula. The young child, only a few hours old, looked delicate and fresh in his mother's arms. He even made the fading paint and dust bunnies on the floor seem clean, like a breath of fresh air just descended on the world and given everything permission to start from scratch once again.

"He's beautiful," Elizabeth said, catching her breath at the sight of him. His head was covered in a thin layer of black hair; his small, fisted hands curled slightly over his swaddling blanket.

Ellen looked up. "Thanks, Lizzie," she said. "This one was the easiest of all. I was in there less than an hour before he came out, dripping with gunk and smelling of roses. I don't know how God does it, but newborns just smell so sweet."

Elizabeth walked over to the side of the bed and stroked her nephew's hair. "May I?" she asked, setting the basket down on the table. Ellen nodded and handed the tiny bundle to her sister. Just like in the first moments she had held her nieces, Elizabeth's heart melted as the small, warm child snuggled close to her and, eyes closed, began the low purr of a newborn. His lips were slightly parted as he breathed in and out, soaking in his first taste of the new world. "How are you feeling?" she asked her sister, still peering down at her nephew.

98 Ellen shifted her weight from her left side to the right in the bed. She

reached a hand out for a glass of ice water and gulped down the remaining liquid. "Exhausted… I had just come home from a shift when I started having contractions. He came so fast I didn't have time to do anything. We barely got to the hospital in time, and Jack had to wait in the lobby with Ivy. There wasn't even time to call a sitter or anything."

"You delivered him alone?" Elizabeth asked, looking up at her sister, gently stroking her nephew's hand.

"Sure," Ellen said. "Jack's no good in the delivery room. With Ivy it would have been easier to not have him there," she laughed and took up her drink once again, only to set it down when she remembered it was empty. "Thanks for coming."

Elizabeth smiled at her sister. "Sure," she said. "It's not every day your sister has a baby."

"It seems like it is with me," Ellen mumbled as she shifted her weight once again. Elizabeth could tell she was uncomfortable in the bed, the pains of childbirth still visible on her face. "You know, I didn't want this child," she said quietly. Elizabeth returned her gaze to her sister and raised her eyebrows. "I told Jack I wanted to end the pregnancy. The thought of another child and dealing with all of that… it was just too much. I'm just so tired of feeling tired, you know?" She looked at her sister.

Elizabeth nodded her head and sighed. "Why did you agree to have another one, sis? Why did Jack want to put you through this again?"

Ellen shrugged and looked away. "I don't know. He's just been different the last few years. Physically, sexually, emotionally… When Ivy was born, it was like he saw her as a fresh start, a chance to make right with life again. And then he drank again and lost his job again. He insisted on another one as if that were his redemption or something, you know. Like having kids was proof his life wasn't a total screw-up."

Elizabeth looked down at Tyson again. Every so often, he would smile lightly, and she could see his eyes rolling back, entering the deep sleep of infancy without a care in the world. "What happens now?" Elizabeth asked gently. "Where do you go from here?"

You know, Lizzie, I look at the two of us and I feel like God has a sense of humor. I was the one with all the promise and the drive. My one weakness has always brought me down, I guess." Lizzie looked at her sister. "I love the wrong men," she said, "and now I've brought two more people into this mess." Elizabeth glanced at her sister who was staring out the window into the winter night. "Sometimes I get so jealous of you, Elizabeth," said Ellen, still staring out the window; a tear slowly making its way down her cheek, landing on the stiff hospital pillow. "I wonder what I could have done to make my life better, to make my life more like yours. I see the way Connor looks at you, like you breathe new life into him every day. Jack has never looked at me that way. Even when we make love, there's shame in his eyes, as if he knows he's going to blow it before he even begins. Do you know what he told me on our wedding night?" Elizabeth shook her head; silent at her sister's abrupt display of emotional depth. "He said, 'If you take care of me, I'm gonna take care of you, baby,' and then jumped on me, so drunk on champagne I could smell it on his collar. What a deal, right?" she grimaced as she looked over at Elizabeth.

Elizabeth furrowed her brow, not quite knowing what to say to her sister. The years had been so hard on her. She was still beautiful, but it was an aging beauty. In moments of stress, Elizabeth could see traces of wrinkles and worry lines starting to appear, marring the once-pristine complexion. Looking down at little Tyson, her heart filled with grief over the boy, the unwanted son of her sister, a child who was pushed into the world half-heartedly. She prayed he never knew the secrets Ellen had revealed tonight. "I don't know what to say, Ellen." She decided the truth was best in the face of her sister's own honesty. "I just don't know what to say," she repeated again, searching for comforting words to share with her sister. "I'm here tonight, sis, and I'll always be here tomorrow." She looked at Ellen who wiped a tear from her face and rolled over on the bed. Glancing at the clock, Elizabeth saw it was almost midnight. She placed the tightly wrapped baby in the bassinet and pulled out the guest bed. There was an old, stained pillow in the closet and a wadded up blanket for overnight guests lying on the bottom shelf. She couldn't help but remember the many nights she had spent in the hospital so many years ago.

Rose lay in the hospital bed, her breathing shallow and sharp as she looked at her daughter. Elizabeth had been holding the mask in place for hours keeping the flow right where it needed to be not trusting the elastic bands to do the work. There was tenderness in her eyes and a slight look of fear as she gazed down at her mother. Rose reached out her hand and placed it over Lizzie's.

"Thank you," she breathed and Elizabeth moved the mask aside.

"You shouldn't waste your time on that," she said. "You need to relax, Mama."

"I want you to know something," Rose said, looking at her daughter. "I want to tell you something before…" Her voice faded.

Elizabeth reached down and stroked her mother's hair. "That's enough of that, Mama," she said. "Whatever you want to tell me can wait until you're better." She placed the mask over her mother's face, but Rose pulled it away.

"I know," she gasped, the words coming between short, raspy breaths, "you are scared. I know you are afraid of being alone. But I want you to know," she gasped again, this time taking longer to regain her strength, "I've loved you more than life itself, baby girl. When you were born, I knew you were going to amaze me. You were going to be my unexpected surprise." Elizabeth reached down and clasped her mother's hand.

"I'm gonna miss you so much, Mama," she said, the sobs coming uncontrollably, shaking both her petite frame and the weak, emaciated body of her mother. "I don't know what I'm going to do without you." The months of sickness washed over her and the façade of strength she had tried so hard to keep came crashing down around her as she let her head drop into her mother's lap. For the first time in weeks, Rose was the one consoling her daughter, rightfully taking her place as a mother. She placed her hands on Elizabeth's head and ran her fingers through her daughter's hair.

Rose took a deep breath and started to sing to her daughter. "You are my sunshine, my little sunshine; you make me happy when skies are grey. You'll never know, dear, how much I love you," she gasped, her voice losing its strength as she fumbled for the oxygen mask.

Elizabeth placed the mask over her mother's face once again. "Please don't take my sunshine away," she finished and watched as her mother slowly slipped away.

Stepping into the bathroom, Elizabeth opened her overnight bag and pulled out her toiletries, lining them up one-by-one on the sink. She went through her nighttime routine and slipped into her flannel pajamas, thankful she brought a warm pair of socks and slippers to shield her feet from the cold hospital floor. When she stepped out of the bathroom, Tyson was stirring in the bassinet, slowly pushing the blankets away from his small frame. She leaned in and picked up her nephew, wrapping the blanket tightly around his body once again. He nuzzled into her chest, moving his head back and forth until he found the perfect little nook to rest in. He closed his eyes.

She eased herself into the rocking chair in the far corner of the room and hummed softly in the baby's ear. She listened as his breathing became rhythmic; once again entering the deep sleep she so envied.

Looking around the room, the maternity ward seemed older than the floor her mother had been on so many years before. Looking down at Tyson, she thought of her mother. This grandchild looked the least like Rose, but Elizabeth could see traces of his grandfather, especially around the lips. She continued rocking in the chair, pulling her robe over the small bundle to add extra warmth in the chill of the winter's night. She pulled the boy closer in and started singing softly in his ear, "You are my sunshine, my little sunshine. You make me happy when skies are grey…"

CHAPTER 19

Elizabeth closed the car door and ran up the apartment steps. The rain was coming down in sheets, soaking her from head to foot in the short run it took her to reach the door. She rang her sister's apartment and heard the buzz of the lock as it was released. "Whew," she said, walking into her sister's place. "It is raining cats and dogs outside. Sorry I'm a little late, but traffic was —" She stopped as she looked around the room. The tension was so thick you could have cut it with a knife. A quick glance at the scene revealed Hannah at the kitchen table, Jack standing in the kitchen doorway and Ellen sitting across from Hannah, holding a screaming Tyson in her arms. Elizabeth walked over and took the infant, kissing him on the head as she fumbled for his pacifier on the table. The soothing motion of the suck calmed him down and he nestled his head into his aunt's chest.

"Where's Ivy?" Elizabeth asked, looking around.

"At a friend's house," said Ellen. Elizabeth felt like an intruder. She had obviously walked into a heated situation but could tell that no one was about to budge.

"Did I miss something?" she asked timidly, looking at her niece across the table.

Ellen motioned for Hannah to speak, "Well? Should you tell her or should I?" Hannah was looking straight into her mother's eyes. Elizabeth was taken aback by the lack of respect she saw sweep across her niece's face. Everything about her was daring her mother to go on.

"Expelled," Ellen finally said. "Expelled from high school with just one year to go."

"Hannah?" Elizabeth gasped. "Is it true?"

Ellen stood up from the table, her hands fisted. "What's the matter with you? You've been expelled. You don't care about anything, especially not me and your father—"

"Step-father," Hannah interrupted, glancing at Jack.

Ellen threw her hands up in the air. "I don't know what to do with you! I see the people you hang out with. If I met them in a dark alley, I would run the other way. They scare the crap out of me, Hannah. You scare the crap out of me! You are ruining your life!"

Hannah sat at the table, motionless, her eyes glaring up at her mother's. "You have no respect for me and no respect for Jack, especially after everything's he's done for you." Hannah muttered something under her breath, and Ellen lost it even more. "What did you say? The least you can do is talk loud enough for me to hear you!" Again, Hannah sat silently, defiance spread across every inch of her face. Ellen sat back down again. "Maybe you can get through to her," she said to Jack.

"I bet you can, you jerk!" Hannah yelled as she rose from the table. "Just leave me alone! All of you," she said, eyeing her aunt, "just leave me alone!" Hannah ran out of the room, the thud of her bedroom door closing echoing throughout the apartment.

"Thanks for the help, Jack," said Ellen sarcastically.

"It's not my fault she's a mess," he said defensively. "I told you we should have done something when she got caught shoplifting. She's out of control, Ellen."

"I don't need *you* to tell me that *my* daughter is out of control! If you weren't such a lazy bas—"

Elizabeth interjected and seemed to startle her sister who, in her anger, had forgotten her sister's presence. "What happened?" she asked.

Ellen forced calmness into her voice. "She hasn't been going to school," she said, glancing at Jack, "for quite some time, evidently. And when she does go, she keeps getting into fights with other students. This last time, she broke some girl's nose, and the school expelled her." Sighing, Ellen placed her head in her hands, rubbing her temples with her index fingers.

Elizabeth sat down next to her sister and kissed Tyson's head once again.

It felt hot, the sweat bumps still formed on his forehead from crying in his mother's arms earlier. "Why don't you let me take Hannah for a few weeks until you figure out what to do." She looked over at Jack, who simply shrugged. He pulled out a cigarette and stepped onto the landing, lighting it up. "Maybe she needs some space."

"It's your funeral," muttered Ellen, regretting the words as soon as she spoke them. "If you can get her to go, then take her."

Elizabeth walked into her sister's bedroom and swayed the small boy back and forth until his eyes started closing. She wiped the snot away from his nose with her shirt and laid him down in the crib at the foot of the bed. Turning off the light, she closed the door behind her and listened for a few moments to make sure the boy was asleep. She took one step across the hall and knocked on Hannah's door. There was no response.

"Hannah," whispered Elizabeth. "It's me, Aunt Lizzie. Can I come in for a second?" She heard the click of the lock and the door opened enough for her to squeeze through. Glancing around, she saw the room was in total disarray. The sheets on the bed were unkempt and stained. It was obvious that someone had been in the bed recently with her niece. Dirty clothes were overflowing in the laundry basket, books and papers scattered about. Looking down at the dresser, Elizabeth noticed a stapled packet titled "Midterm" on the front with a red "F" penciled underneath the words. "See me after class," someone had scrawled under the lettering.

Hannah reached over and grabbed the packet. "That teacher hated me," she said. "Before I even started his fuc—" she caught herself in the presence of her aunt, "stupid class, he hated me."

"Hannah, I have a proposition," said Elizabeth, choosing to lean on the dresser rather than sit on the bed. "I want you to come and live with us again, just for a few weeks, until you and your parents figure out what the next step is."

Hannah eyed her aunt. "If my mom doesn't want me here, then I have friends, you know," she said. "You don't have to take me in."

"That's right," said Elizabeth. "I don't have to do anything for you. But I want to." She looked at her niece. "What do you say?"

This time it was Hannah who looked away, unable to match her aunt's *105* gaze. "Sure," she said. "I mean, it's only for a few weeks. I promise I won't get into any trouble while I'm there."

Elizabeth grabbed a few things off the dresser and started stuffing them in a duffel bag. "I'm not worried so much about that," she said and placed the duffel bag on the bed. "I'll be waiting in the living room. Take all the time you need."

As Elizabeth pulled into their garage, she could only think what Connor would say when he saw her once again unloading her niece's luggage into the kitchen. As she walked in the door, a surprised Connor looked out from the refrigerator where he'd been rummaging around for food. "Hey!" he said, surprised. "I thought you were babysitting tonight." She walked over and kissed him, gently touching his arm.

"Hannah's going to be staying with us for a while," she said. If he showed any signs of question or concern, he hid them well, looking over his wife's shoulder and welcoming his niece once again into his home.

"Hey, Hannah," he called, pulling out a diet soda from the fridge. "I was just going to throw together a bachelor-esque dinner. Want some?" Hannah looked over at her aunt and uncle, their faces reflecting off the polished microwave door. This world seemed so foreign to her, even though she had been here only a few months before, waiting out the weeks before Tyson's birthday. She stood on the linoleum, a frail, pale figure looking out of place amidst the luxury that surrounded her.

"I'm not that hungry," she said. "If you don't mind, I think I'll just go to my room." Not waiting for them to reply, she hauled her stuff down the hall and into the guest room that had been her sanctuary.

Connor handed Elizabeth mayonnaise and mustard, himself pulling the cold cuts and lettuce out of the fridge. "Well?" he said. "What's going on?"

Elizabeth sat the condiments on the counter and walked over to the pantry to get the bread. "She's been expelled, Connor," she said. He stopped midway through opening the jar and looked at his wife.

"Excuse me?"

"I know," said Elizabeth. "I couldn't believe it either. It's two weeks from the end of her junior year and it's over. She's done."

"What the hell happened?" he asked, still too shocked to finish his sandwich.

"She hasn't been going to school and she's been getting into fights. If I could turn back time," she said, opening the bread bag, "I would have never dropped her off at home after Tyson was born. She was just starting to change, and we sent her home again."

"What did Jack have to say?"

"What do you think?" said Elizabeth, her disgust for her brother-in-law evident in her tone. "Nothing. He just lit up a cigarette and walked outside, leaving Ellen to deal with the mess."

Connor spread the mayonnaise onto his bread, slapped on a few slices of turkey, and placed the top of his sandwich back on, noticeably distracted. "I don't understand it, Elizabeth. He used to really care for her, and now it's like she's live-in help or something. Somewhere along the line, they just started hating each other."

"Somewhere along the line, I started hating him, too," said Elizabeth, feeling childish as she said it aloud. "He's not that easy to love."

Connor reached down and made another sandwich, this time adding the lettuce and cheese. He placed it and a small handful of chips on a plate and, grabbing a soda as he passed the fridge, he walked to his niece's room. He knocked on her door. "It's me. It's Uncle Connor."

Hannah began apologizing as she opened the door and stopped as she saw the food in his arms. He looked like an Indian bringing a peace offering to the troops. "I know you said you weren't hungry, but you're skin and bones, and if I were you, I'd be starving." He placed the food on the dresser right inside the door and respectfully stepped back out into the hallway. "You know we love you, Hannah," he said gently. "Let us know if you need anything."

Hannah watched him walk away until he rounded the corner and she could hear the low murmurings of him and her aunt in the kitchen. Her bag buzzed on the floor and she fumbled around for her cell phone. Ignoring the call, she placed it on the bedside table. She recognized the name as that of a boy from school she had recently hooked up with. In the sanctuary of her aunt's bedroom, she embraced the distance between her and the drama going on just a few miles across town.

She glanced over at the plate of food her uncle had left. She had to admit that she was hungry and she gobbled it up, leaving only a few crumbs on the plate. She hadn't eaten all day and she had been out late the night before at a party. Not having anything to eat or drink since the cold beers last night was making her feel nauseous.

In the moonlight, the room had a soft glow. Her aunt had hung a new picture, a simple embroidery with the words *Faith, Hope and Love*, over the bed. Looking closer, Hannah saw that it must have been her grandmother's, as the name "Rose" was scribbled in permanent marker in the lower right hand corner of the piece. She opened her bag and began filling the drawers once again, feeling both a sense of failure and déjà vu as she unloaded her things.

CHAPTER 20

"Hannah? Are you okay?"

Hannah lifted her head from the bathroom floor. The cold tile felt good as she wretched into the toilet, her head spinning. The weeks at her aunt and uncle's house felt like she had won the lottery. For the first time since Tyson was born, Hannah felt like she could sleep uninterrupted. There was no avoiding her stepfather and no walking on eggshells around her mother. It just felt safe, and she hadn't felt safe since the last time she stayed with them.

"I'm fine," she called out. "I must have eaten something that didn't agree with me." She fell back down on the tile and lifted herself to the toilet bowl once again as the nausea swept over her. The room was slowly spinning as she reached a hand up and flushed the toilet once more. The door clicked open and her aunt walked into the bathroom.

"I'm so sorry. Please don't think I'm intruding, but if you're sick, I need to help you," she said, reaching down and handing her niece a cold washcloth. "Here, let me pull your hair back for you." She gently tied Hannah's hair back into a ponytail and sat down next to her on the floor. "Can you make it to your bed, at least?" Hannah nodded and allowed her aunt to guide her along like a little child. They reached the bed and Elizabeth tucked her in, even fluffing the pillows for her. "I'm calling the doctor," she said resolutely after returning with a cup of water.

"I'm fine, really," Hannah said, sitting up in bed. "Besides, it's after nine o'clock and I know you have worked today."

Elizabeth shook her head. "Uh-uh. I already called in and took a personal day. I'll call Dr. Monroe, and hopefully she has an opening. She usually 109 keeps days open for stuff like this." Hannah finally conceded and lay back in bed.

By the time they arrived at Dr. Monroe's office, Hannah was already feeling better. She tried to convince her aunt it was probably just food poisoning, but Lizzie would have none of it. She insisted they keep the appointment just to make sure everything was okay. Dr. Monroe did some tests, took some blood work and, after asking Hannah for a urine sample, left them alone for a few minutes.

"I still think this is silly," Hannah said, looking at her aunt. Elizabeth rolled her eyes.

"You are as stubborn as your mother," she said. "Drop it. She would have lain in bed half dead before she would get up and go to the doctor. Do you know how much aspirin that woman consumed as a teenager?" Hannah laughed. Things with Aunt Liz were so laid back compared to things with her mother. Mom was always working or tired from working, and even something as simple as a doctor's appointment would have eventually turned into an argument. It was nice to have normalcy for a change.

Dr. Monroe stepped back in and looked at Elizabeth. "Elizabeth, since you are not the mother, I'm going to need you to step out while I read Hannah her test results."

"I'm sure Hannah won't mind," she said, looking at her niece. Hannah shook her head and was about to speak when Dr. Monroe interrupted.

"Actually, it's not an option, I'm afraid. Please wait outside and I'll come and get you when we're ready." Hannah glanced at her aunt and saw her expression had changed. There were lines on her forehead and she could tell she was worried. Hannah felt okay until she noticed her aunt's expression. As her aunt got up and walked toward the door, a sinking feeling entered Hannah's stomach. When the door closed after Elizabeth, Dr. Monroe looked back at Hannah and pulled her chair closer. "How old are you?" she asked gently.

"I'm seventeen," said Hannah, "but I've already told you that." The doctor's demeanor was making Hannah even more nervous.

Dr. Monroe ignored her comment. "When was your last period?"

Hannah narrowed her eyes. "Why?" she asked.

"Because, Hannah," she said, sighing before she finished the sentence, "you're pregnant. About six weeks along." Hannah sat and stared at the doctor. It felt like she was in a fog, and the words of Dr. Monroe sounded hollow as they rang through her ears.

"But I…" she stammered. " How did this happen?" She pulled her arms into her and folded them across her chest. Despair flooded her body and she slowly sank into the hopelessness she was feeling.

"I know it's a shock, Hannah, but I ran the test twice, just to make sure. Maybe we should call your mother." Dr. Monroe stopped talking and was looking at her. "Did you hear what I said, Hannah?" Hannah shook her head once more. "I asked you if you want me to call your mother. It's not mandatory, but it might be a good idea. "

"No," Hannah blurted out. "No, I don't want to call my mother." Once again, Dr. Monroe stopped and stared at the young girl. Hannah wished she would go away. She wished everything and everyone would just go away.

"All right," she finally said. "Do you want me to get your aunt?"

"Yes," she whispered, "and I would like for you to tell her, if you don't mind." Hannah didn't have the guts to tell her aunt the news. Elizabeth had just been saying how proud she was of Hannah since she'd come to live with them. The shame lay on Hannah's face like a blanket. She pulled her legs up in the chair and listened as Dr. Monroe paged her aunt to return to the room.

Elizabeth poked her head inside the door, looking even more worried than before, as she saw her niece huddled like a frightened animal on her chair. She sat down on the empty seat next to Hannah and put her arm around her shoulders. Hannah felt horrible at what was meant to be a kind gesture. She closed her eyes; wishing she could fade away somewhere far away from her aunt's loving pull.

"Elizabeth," Dr. Monroe began, "the tests we performed on Hannah showed everything was fine…"

"Oh, thank goodness," breathed Elizabeth. "I was so afraid something was terribly wrong, especially given our family history," she said, wiping away a tear of relief. She looked down at Hannah, who still had her eyes closed, and glanced at Dr. Monroe, who didn't seem excited at the good news. "I'm sorry," she said. "I thought you said everything was fine?"

"Yes, everything is fine, except for one thing. Hannah is six weeks pregnant." The silence that filled the room was unbearable. Hannah flinched as her aunt removed her arm from her shoulder. There was a weight in the absence of her aunt's touch.

"I see," said Lizzie. "What do we do now?"

Dr. Monroe took out a business card and handed it to Elizabeth, "She needs to see an OB/GYN immediately. I don't know if she has insurance or not "Elizabeth shook her head. " Then there are options for that, too, since she's a minor. We didn't discuss who the father is, but there are decisions that need to be made." Elizabeth sat in the chair, her arms full of the brochures and business cards Dr. Monroe had been handing her as she spoke. "I'll leave you two alone." She stepped out of the room and Hannah could hear the drop of the chart into the bin outside the door.

Elizabeth reached over and grabbed her niece's hand. "Hannah?" she said softly. "Please open your eyes. It's going to be okay." She wasn't expecting the kind words from her aunt, and the compassion opened a flood of tears. She sat in the chair, her body heaving as the sobs made the chair quiver on the linoleum floor. It all seemed so hopeless as she thought of the last time she had unprotected sex. She thought of her stepfather the night Tyson was born. The pain of the past years suddenly overwhelmed her small frame, and she couldn't stop the hysterics from mounting. Memories of her liaisons while living at home in the months following his birth raced across her mind; the countless number of boys from school she had used to fuel the increasing numbness. The frequency of her stepfather's visits as she, now a teenager, found herself using him, almost taunting him, daring him to approach for every encounter.

She felt dirty. As her aunt embraced her and her perfume wafted over her, she felt cheap and disgusting. "I'm sorry," she finally managed to say to her aunt. "I'm just so sorry, Aunt Liz." The salty taste of tears fell into her mouth as she spoke the apology. Elizabeth shushed her and, reaching down and lifting the girl's face, said reassuringly, "That's enough. We've had our pity party, and now it's time to be a big girl," she told her niece, echoing the words her own mother had said so many times to her. "We're going to go home and think about what to do."

The ride home was spent in silence except for the radio music playing in the background. Hannah was grateful for the distraction. When they stepped inside the house, Hannah looked around and suddenly the familiar seemed foreign. It hit her she would probably have to leave her aunt's home. She had always known this would happen eventually, but she had almost begun to believe this fantasy world would go on forever.

"How about some coffee?" Elizabeth asked. She reached into the cabinet and pulled out the bag. As she was about to pour it into the coffee maker, she stopped. She placed the bag back in the cabinet and opted for the de-caffeinated blend instead. Her fingers fumbled on the machine until eventually the percolation sent a comforting aroma throughout the kitchen. Opening the fridge, she pulled out the remains of a pound cake and set it on the table. Hannah didn't need an invitation to sit down.

"You know, when your grandmother died, there was so much food in our house it almost seemed sick. I was so overcome with grief that every cake, every casserole, every bottle of soda pop seemed profane, almost sacrilegious to me. But now, I kind of understand," she said, cutting two pieces of the cake and placing them onto napkins. "There's something soothing about food. It's almost a sign that life goes on." Then, Elizabeth looked over at her niece, waiting for Hannah to explain.

"I, um…" Hannah fumbled for the words. She felt the internal pull to tell her aunt of the horrors of her past and was desperately fighting against sharing what for so long had been her dirty little secret. She had held onto the lies and the secrecy for so long she almost convinced herself it was no big deal. "I just want to say thank you for everything you've done… "Elizabeth held a hand to stop her niece."

"No, we're not doing this like that," she said. "This is not a relationship ender, Hannah. We're not sending you away." The girls' eyes filled with tears as she looked down at the table, her left hand carelessly holding the napkin-wrapped piece of cake.

"I'm just so sorry." Hannah didn't bother wiping away her tears.

Elizabeth sighed and set her coffee mug down. "Hannah, you never really knew your grandmother," she began. "I don't know if you knew this, but she got pregnant with your mother before she married your grandfather." Hannah raised her eyebrows as she looked at her aunt. "She loved our father, for what good it did her, but the pregnancy was the main reason they got hitched." She looked over at her niece and smiled. "The reason I'm telling you this is because I always felt like my mother saw herself as a second-class citizen because of that one mistake. She raised us to believe we could do and be anything, and I watched as the women at church made snide comments or conveniently forgot to call her for certain meetings. Your Grandma Rose carried that shame like a weight around her neck all her life. And if she were here today…" Elizabeth's voice broke off as she stopped to regain her composure, "I'm pretty sure she would tell you life is too short to wake up every day feeling like a failure."

"I don't remember her," said Hannah. "All I have is a picture of her and me together just a few days before she died."

"She was an amazing woman," Elizabeth said as she wiped her eyes once more with a tissue. "I have to remind myself not to idolize her, though, because she could be one pain in the butt if she wanted to be, don't get me wrong." She laughed at the memory.

"I'm scared," whispered Hannah. "I'm scared of talking to my mom. Can you tell her for me?"

"Oh, honey," said Elizabeth affectionately. "I can't walk that road for you. Your mother, she…" she fumbled for the right words, and continued, "Let's just say she had a different dream for her life than the one she's living today. She always knew she would be something, and when life took her another direction, I don't think she knew how to handle it. She loves you though, Hannah," added Elizabeth. "She really does love you."

Hannah stiffened in her chair; doubt filling her as her aunt spoke the words again. She hadn't even talked to her mother in over three weeks. The thought of her mother loving her was a reality she had let go of long ago. On most days, it seemed like they tolerated each other. "I'll tell her," said Hannah as she bit into her cake. "I'll tell her what's going on," she said awkwardly.

"Hannah, I hate to mention this, but do you know who the father is?"

Hannah felt the old numbness returning as her aunt spoke the words. The truth was she had no idea. Almost six weeks ago to the day, she had lain under the weight of her stepfather as he used her for his own pleasure, then got up and left; leaving her alone and frightened on her bed. The next day, out of sheer retaliation, she slept with a boy from third period just to irk her stepfather, intentionally scheduling the encounter so Jack would see him walk out of her room as he came home from work. Hannah closed her eyes, suppressing the thoughts and feelings of what had happened that night; hating her body for reacting physically to the memories.

Hannah shook her head. "No, I don't. Things were… confusing then," she finally said. She longed for her aunt to dismiss her so she could retreat to her room.

"Let's deal with that later, then," Elizabeth said. "I'll tell your Uncle Connor when he gets home, and we'll invite your mom and Jack over for dinner this weekend. Why don't you get some rest?" Hannah walked into her room and closed the door. Sliding down onto the hardwood floor, she sat staring into nothing until she saw the sky darken outside her window.

CHAPTER 21

Hannah was helping her aunt set the table for dinner when she heard the car door slam and the doorbell ring. She felt sick to her stomach as she listened to her uncle greet her mother and stepfather. Elizabeth walked over and kissed her on the back of the head, handing her the silverware. "I know it seems bad now," said Elizabeth, "but soon it will all be over."

The week since she first found out had been a whirlwind. Her aunt had taken more time off to take Hannah to the obstetrician who would be delivering the baby. So far, the baby looked healthy and, even though she had seen the small heartbeat on the sonogram, Hannah still felt a sense of detachment. Knowing her grandmother, mother, and now she herself had all gone through the same situation was not comforting; it was confusing. She couldn't help but think the only reason Aunt Lizzie had come through unscathed was because she couldn't have children. She envied her.

Ellen came into the room and nodded at her daughter. Hannah stiffened as her stepfather gave her shoulder a tug and kissed her on the forehead. "I miss you," he whispered in her ear.

The roast cooking in the oven finished on time, so the usual before-dinner chitchat was thankfully avoided.

"Jack, how's work going?" asked Connor in a feeble attempt at trying to lighten the mood.

"It's not going," he said, grabbing more than his share of mashed potatoes. "Those morons fired me last week. I'm done with it. I think I'll start out on my own." Ellen rolled her eyes as she took the plate of mashed potatoes from Jack.

"Oh, sorry to hear that," said Connor, not knowing where else to take the 117 conversation.

Elizabeth cleared her throat and looked at Hannah out of the corner of her eye. She was staring at her dinner plate. "Well, I guess you've wondered why we asked you over tonight."

"You're my sister," Ellen said coldly. "I don't have expectations." She was staring straight at her daughter. "But I'm assuming it's because Hannah is ready to apologize, and quite frankly, I don't think I can… "

"Liz," interrupted her sister, "it's not that."

Ellen looked at Elizabeth with raised eyebrows, as if to say, "What, then?"

Elizabeth continued, "Hannah does, however, have something she would like to say." She nodded to Hannah, her nonverbal queue that it was time to tell her mother.

For a split second, Hannah thought of running out the back door, jumping the fence and never returning. Instead, she simply said, "I'm pregnant," in a tone so quiet it was barely audible. The room fell silent. Ellen was staring at her daughter, her eyes slanted, and Jack's fork was caught in mid-air.

"Excuse me," said Ellen, "I don't think I heard you correctly. You're what?"

"I'm pregnant, Mom," Hannah said again. "You, more than anyone else, should know the meaning of that word." Hannah couldn't help but add the extra sting.

Ellen stared at her daughter for what seemed like minutes and then reached across the table and slapped her across the face. "You little slut!" she yelled, making her way around the table. "How could you do this to me, to yourself?"

Elizabeth jumped up, prepared to block her sister from reaching her daughter, when Hannah burst out, "If I'm the slut, maybe it's because your dear hubby made me one!" Hannah screamed the words; one hand placed over her cheek, still stinging from her mother's attack, the other pointing accusingly at Jack. This time, it was Connor who broke the silence.

"Hannah," he said cautiously, "what do you mean?"

"Tell, them, Jack, how you've been having your way with me," she said. "Tell them!" she screamed, tears streaming down her face. She looked around at the shocked faces and couldn't control the sobs and the words as they came pouring out of her. "He went down on me, Mama," she cried. "He went down on me on the night of my twelfth birthday. Then he kept coming at me. He even did it here at Aunt Liz's house. Then he started having his way with me. Mama, I swear I didn't know how to stop it! For five years, you ruined my life!" she yelled, her finger still pointed at her stepfather.

For a moment, it seemed as if time had frozen as the news of her confession cut through the air. When the words sunk in, Connor lunged at Jack, punching him in the face and pinning him to the floor. "You bastard! I'm going to kill you!" he yelled, hitting him in the nose again and again. "I'll kill you, you pervert!"

"Get off me!" yelled Jack, pushing Connor off and struggling back to his feet. He looked imploringly at Ellen and then at Hannah, wringing his hand and fumbling for a cigarette in his pocket. "Are you gonna believe her? Let's go," he said desperately, gathering up his jacket and Ellen's purse.

"Jack," Ellen whispered, "is it true? Did you touch my baby girl?" Ellen approached her husband, the look of shock still written all over her face. "Did you touch my baby girl?" He said nothing. "Did you touch my baby girl!" she yelled, throwing her fists against his chest, her hands clawing at his face. Jack grabbed her wrists, once again pushing his attacker off.

"What do you think?" he yelled at Ellen, his strong hands around her wrists. "You're going to believe her, after the lies and crap she's already put you through?"

His nose was bleeding from Connor's punches, and there was a look of panic on his face as he surveyed the crowd. Hannah's sobs filled the room, her body convulsing, racking under the freedom she felt as the shame was finally lifted from her. "We didn't do anything wrong," he said, desperation filling his face. "She's my daughter, Ellen. I'm telling you the truth; I've always loved her as my own." He looked around again, scanning the faces for any signs of mercy. He received none. "I always loved you, baby," he said to Ellen, pulling her close to him and stroking her face with his hands. "This was just a thing between us. She…" he fought for the words. "She enticed me," he finally said, his words sounding angry. "You think she's all innocent in this, huh? Think of all the guys she's been with, all the boys we've caught her with," he said, again looking at Ellen, hoping to win her over to his side *119* with his feeble attempt at justification. The room fell silent, filled only with the Hannah's sobs as her aunt held her.

"That's it!" yelled Connor, again flying at Jack. This time, Jack was ready, and the punches and hits were returned. It was Ellen who eventually pulled Connor off and away.

"Enough!" she yelled, her eyes fixated on Connor, daring him to move again. "If you make one more move," she threatened her brother-in-law, "I'm calling the police!" Everyone in the room froze.

"Ellen!" Elizabeth said. "You can't be serious. You believe him?" she asked accusingly. "You believe him over your own daughter?" Everyone's eyes were on Ellen as she coolly picked her purse up from the floor and started towards her daughter.

"I've tried with you," she said in a low voice, trying hard to keep her cool. "God knows I've tried. I've given you chance after chance to make things right with us. You've broken the law, you've had boys over to our apartment, you got kicked out of school," she grabbed her daughter's wrist. "I even tried to be understanding when you came home with tattoos," she said, flinging her daughter violently away. "But this," Ellen was fighting back tears, "this is too much."

Hannah stood up tall against her mother, the young girl's silhouette strengthened by her confession. "I don't care if you believe me," she said, nodding at Jack. "He knows the truth. If you want to sleep with a child molester, then…" Ellen slapped her daughter across the face. This time it was Elizabeth who stepped between them.

"I think you should leave," she told her sister. "I think we all need time to clear our heads." Ellen walked past her sister and Elizabeth grabbed her arm. "I think you need time to *think* about this," she emphasized, looking intently in her sister's eyes, pleading with her to reconsider.

As Jack followed his wife from the room, he passed Connor, who grabbed him by the throat and pinned him against the wall. "Get out," he said, through clenched teeth. "Get out of my house. If you ever so much as breathe on anyone in this family again, make no mistake about it, I will kill you." He released his grip and pushed Jack towards the front door, slamming it behind the couple. He leaned back against the door and listened as Jack sped away. More than anything, his head was reeling from the evening, trying to sort through what had just taken place in his home.

Walking into the kitchen, Connor found Hannah and Elizabeth crumpled on the kitchen floor. Elizabeth ran over to him and fell into his chest, her sobs soaking his shirt as he tried to soothe her.

Connor finally broke the silence. "Hannah," he said gently, "I think we should go to the police, right now. If Jack did this to you, he might do it to your sister," he said, hating the words as they came from his mouth. He felt dirty for even thinking about what that monster might do.

Hannah shook her head firmly. "No," she said, "he wouldn't hurt them, not his own flesh and blood. I don't want to go to the police. They wouldn't believe me either." Elizabeth let go of Connor and walked over to her niece. She cupped Hannah's face in her hands and looked down at the young girl who, for once, looked like the fragile teenager that she was.

"We believe you," she said firmly, "and we'll support your decisions about Jack, about the baby – about everything."

"Aunt Lizzie," Hannah spoke, her voice shaking as she tried to hold back the tears, "I'm so scared. I'm so sorry I didn't tell you sooner. I was so afraid," she sobbed as her apology came forth, speaking about things over which she had so little control. "I don't know whose baby this is. It could be some boy at school, or it could be…" her voice trailed off, as she looked away, fearful of meeting her aunt's gaze. Elizabeth wiped the tears from her eyes, taking a deep breath to garner what little strength she had left.

"We'll cross that bridge when we come to it," she said. Elizabeth reached down and, grabbing her niece's chin, forced Hannah to look her in the eyes. "You don't have to do anything you don't want to do. Do you understand?" Hannah nodded, grateful her aunt was trying to comfort her, but falling into the hopelessness, she felt inside. The tears came once more, surprising Hannah at their intensity, at the fact she had any tears left to give.

"Hush," Elizabeth said, pulling the girl off the floor. "It's been a crazy night. I think we should all go to sleep, and tomorrow we'll figure out what to do."

They watched as Hannah walked down the hallway; sitting silently at the table, listening as she took a shower, brushed her teeth and then finally *121* seemed to fall asleep. Connor looked at his wife, wishing he had the right words to comfort her. There were mascara lines down her cheeks; signs of the sorrow that filled her eyes. He reached over and placed his hand over hers; waiting for her to speak or ready to sit in silence if that's what she needed.

"Sometimes," she began slowly, "I still feel like that frightened girl sitting in that tenement, all alone and scared."

Connor squeezed her hand. "You're not that person anymore, Elizabeth. You are so much stronger now."

"I used to lie in bed at night with my eyes clenched tight, and have pretend conversations with my mom. I would picture her lying beside me on the bed, on her side, propped up like she used to do, just talking to me about my day." Elizabeth was staring off, her eyes glazed over. "Life is so much pain," she whispered. "When Mama died, I didn't know if I could take any more pain. Haven't we had our share?" She looked at her husband, feeling guilty as soon as she saw the worried look on his face.

"We'll figure this out," he said. "We'll figure this out."

CHAPTER 22

The months following Hannah's confession seemed to drag on, gruelingly slow for Elizabeth, Hannah, and Connor. Heaviness hung over the house as Hannah's body continued to grow and change an everyday reminder of the situation at hand. It had been months since Elizabeth heard from her sister. There had been no word since that evening that changed things for the entire family. Elizabeth knew even if Ellen eventually reached out to her daughter, the damage had already been done.

Hannah's strength and renewed sense of purpose made Elizabeth even surer there confession was true. She had been a different person since finally confronting her stepfather, a weight lifted from her shoulders, giving her the freedom to live. Hannah successfully completed her GED and was already looking into study programs in the fall. Even though Connor and Elizabeth knew this was unrealistic with the coming baby, they couldn't bring themselves to broach the subject with Hannah. It was like the girl was living in a dream world, unable to accept and face the reality that the child growing inside of her could possibly be Jack's.

Elizabeth was home alone with her niece while Connor was away on a business trip. She enjoyed the one-on-one time with Hannah, treasuring the closeness she felt. For the first time in her life, she felt more like a mother than an aunt. She tried to remind herself Hannah was not her own, but she couldn't help but step in and fill that role.

Elizabeth could never bring herself to ask Hannah about her pregnancy. She found herself walking on eggshells around the topic; afraid to bring it up around her niece lest it spoil the fantasyland it seemed all of them had a part in creating. She hadn't been to any doctor's appointments since the first one and was still trying to wear her old clothes, which had only recently started becoming too tight. Hannah was even making jokes about her weight gain, trying to fool herself into believing it would all just go away.

It was Dr. Monroe who finally brought Elizabeth back to reality. She called to see why Hannah had missed her last two appointments, reminding Elizabeth of the importance of early care, especially with a young mother. As Elizabeth looked over at her niece, she knew they could no longer live in denial. Hannah was pregnant. The baby might be her step-fathers. This was their new reality.

Hannah was leaning over the fridge, intently looking at its contents; feeling as if she were eating for the tenth time today. "Got any mayo?" she asked.

Elizabeth looked up from the table and pushed her laptop away. "No, I think we're out," she said, summoning the courage to speak with her niece.

"That's too bad, because I had a craving for a turkey and Swiss sandwich on rye bread. Funny, isn't it, because I've never really liked rye bread, but…"

"Dr. Monroe called today," Elizabeth interrupted, the words sounding too harsh and too loud, making them even more uncomfortable.

"Oh?" Hannah said. "What did she want?"

"She said she was concerned for the baby because you were missing your appointments." Elizabeth looked at her niece, waiting for her to react. "She said early prenatal care is really important, and you really should be coming in." She waited for her niece to speak.

"I really wish we had mayo," Hannah said, sticking her head back in the fridge. "I can't stand mustard these days." Elizabeth walked over to her niece and gently started closing the refrigerator door.

"Hannah," she said calmly, "I think we should talk. You are pregnant. You can't change that. I can't change that. But we should take care of the baby."

"We?" Hannah questioned. "You said 'we' should take care of the baby. Last time I checked, this wasn't your baby." Elizabeth stopped and stared at her niece. Tough conversations with Hannah reminded her more than ever of conversations with her sister. At the drop of a hat, either one could turn on you, the survival instinct kicking into overdrive.

"I know it's your baby. And I also know you probably don't want to think about it, but you can't make this go away. So do you want to call Dr. Monroe, or should I?"

Hannah looked down at the floor while her aunt stood leaning against the fridge. "I hit myself sometimes," she said quietly. "Sometimes at night, I start thinking about my baby and about Jack, and I start to hit my stomach." She continued staring at the floor, a single tear beginning to fall down her face. "I hit myself and then I get mad that I don't have the courage to hit myself harder. And then I think what kind of a loser am I that I couldn't stop Jack from raping me? And now I don't even have the guts to end this baby's life. And then I feel mad that I want to end a baby's life. What kind of a person wants to kill their baby?" she asked, finally looking up at her aunt.

Elizabeth stared at her niece, instinctively reaching out to pull her hair from her face. "What Jack did to you was wrong. I don't know if there's a single right reaction to all of this. But we can't ignore it and we can't make it go away, Hannah. Hurting your baby won't solve anything."

Hannah nodded. "I'll call Dr. Monroe tomorrow. Aunt Lizzie?"

"Yes?"

"I don't know if I want this baby," she said slowly, her voice barely a whisper. "I don't mean I want to terminate it," she said quickly, "but what if I gave it away?"

Elizabeth tried to speak but stopped as her own tears choked her voice, "That," she cleared her throat. "That's your choice. If you decide that's what you want to do, then we'll help you. Now, how about we go to the store and hook you up with some mayonnaise?" Hannah smiled at her aunt and nodded.

Elizabeth hesitated before walking up the stone steps. Her mind reeled as she stood before the grey building and emotions flooded her. She had never actually been to the office, since an Internet search had been enough to find her a reputable investigator. Up until this moment, it didn't seem real. Even signing the first check over and putting it in the mail was still, a safe distance from whatever this man may uncover about her brother-in-law.

She pressed the buzzer for the suite and a gruff voice spoke to her through *125* the intercom. "Hello?"

"H-hello," she stammered. "This is Elizabeth. Elizabeth Templeton. I have a meeting with you today."

"Oh, yeah, come on up," he said, and the door buzzed for her to enter. She walked up a short flight of stairs and found herself outside the door of what seemed like an old-fashioned business suite. The gold and black lettering on the door read "George Exeter, Private Investigator." There was nothing fancy, nothing overrated. It was all simple and straight-forward. Stepping into the office, she didn't expect to see anyone else and was surprised to see a young woman sitting behind what appeared to be a receptionist desk. She smiled at Elizabeth and placed her hand over the phone receiver.

"It's just through that door," she said politely and continued her conversation. Elizabeth stepped into the office just to the left of the desk and was again rather surprised by the man who greeted her.

"Mrs. Templeton," he said and held out his hand. Elizabeth shook the hand of a rather young man with a deceptively harsh voice. He was very well put together; his appearance looked more like that of a businessperson than of a private investigator. He was well groomed and offered her a soda before they started their meeting. She politely refused and sat down, still nervous about the encounter. "Well, I remember the last time we spoke; you mentioned your niece was living with you. Is that still the situation?

Elizabeth nodded. "Yes. She's due in a couple of months with the baby."

"I'm glad to hear that," said George. "About her living situation, I mean. The fact is, Elizabeth…" He stopped and looked at her. "May I call you Elizabeth?'

"Of course."

"I've uncovered some rather disturbing things about Jack Edwards. Before I give you this information, I just want to warn you that your worst fears are probably true in this situation. I've done the investigative work, and at this point all I can do is hand it over to you and walk away. I am not responsible for what you do with this information. Are we in agreement?"

Elizabeth tried to keep her cool, although she couldn't help from nervously tapping her foot against the floor. "I understand."

George nodded and, sitting down at his desk, handed her a manila envelope, himself opening what appeared to be a duplicate of the one she was holding. "This is not Jack's first offence," he said. "Before he married your sister, he was dating a young woman in Cincinnati. The woman had a daughter who eventually accused Jack of the same thing. The daughter had a child and claimed the baby was Jack's. They never turned Jack over to the police, so he got away and moved to Chicago. That was the only case I could find." He stopped and looked at Elizabeth.

"Is there something else?" Elizabeth questioned.

George sighed and closed the folder. "I normally don't get involved beyond divulging information, Mrs. Templeton, but I can't help but voice my opinion on this one. If what you are saying about your niece is true, and if what this woman is accusing Jack of is true, then at some point, this has to stop. Look," he said, rubbing his temples and loosening his tie, "my father was a police officer, so were my grandfather and my older brother. I looked at the life they led, feeling as if all they were doing was recycling criminals into a broken system, only to arrest them again when the system failed to prosecute. I chose a different route because I didn't want the same despondency. Ethically, all I am supposed to do is investigate, give you information, and walk away. This one is tough, though, because I have a daughter, too, and if any jerk ever touched my daughter, there's no way I'd let him off easy. That's all I'm saying."

"I understand," Elizabeth said, staring at the contents of the folder.

"Hopefully I didn't come across as too preachy," George said, smiling; trying to make the mood somewhat light-hearted. "This was a tough one, Elizabeth. Most of my clients are rich wives who suspect their husbands of cheating. I was hoping I would find happier news for you. I'm so sorry."

Elizabeth looked at the young man, really looked at him for the first time. He already had shoots of grey, giving him a premature salt and pepper look. Although his clothes were clean and well pressed, they were also well worn, bearing the marks of someone who works hard but didn't reap the financial benefits. Elizabeth thought of how lucky his little girl was to have such a father. "I really do appreciate your work," she said, looking at him straight in the eye. "I understand all that you've said. No offence, but hopefully we'll never have to meet again." *127*

George nodded and stood up as she did, respectfully, like a well-brought-up young man. "That would be my hope as well. And Elizabeth," he held out his hand once more, "go in peace." His words startled Elizabeth. She shook his hand quickly and left the office without returning the goodbye of the young receptionist. Walking outside, the cold Chicago wind hit her smack in the face. The city was already preparing for winter, and pedestrians had their coats pulled tight; collars upturned as they hurried to bus and train stops.

She boarded a bus herself, taking the last open seat. Staring out the window, she wondered about her sister, still perplexed at the sudden lack of communication and distance she had imposed on their relationship. Things in their family had changed overnight, and more than anything she wished she could turn back the hand of time to when Ellen first told her about Jack. She had lacked so little courage then and had grown so much in the years since their mother's death.

She watched as blocks passed and passengers got on and off. As the bus let her off near her house, she looked resolutely ahead of her and knew one thing to be true: more than anything, she needed to go to Cincinnati.

CHAPTER 23

"Cincinnati?" Connor looked at his wife as if she had just lost her mind. "What are you thinking? Why is this the first time you're telling me any of this?"

Elizabeth felt sick. She knew from the beginning she should have let her husband know about the investigator, about her suspicions, but something inside retreated from him rather than choosing to trust. She opened her mouth to speak and tears came to her eyes. "I'm so sorry, Connor," she said, sitting down on the bed. "I should have told you." Instead of approaching his wife, Connor kept his distance, knowing if he walked over to console her, all of his nerve would be lost.

"We're talking about private detectives, meetings held in secret without telling me. What were you thinking, Elizabeth?"

"I don't know what I was thinking. I just had a hunch there was more to Jack. So I hired the guy and went to his office and that's when I found out about Christina. There's nothing more to it. I swear."

"I get that things are tough, Liz," he said, "but we can't have the chaos of your sister's life ruin ours. I'm on your side, Liz, I really am, but going all the way to Cincinnati to look for a woman who may or may not have had Jack's baby sounds a little crazy. I mean, what are you going to say to her when you find her? 'Hello, do you know Jack? He raped my niece and now he's having his baby.' Is there any kind of a plan?"

"I don't know," Elizabeth said, sensing that the answer lacked the surety he needed to hear from her. "I have no idea whatsoever, Connor. All I know is if I don't go, I'll always wonder."

"That's because you've opened Pandora's Box! You should have never let it 129 get this far. Hannah needs you here. The baby is due soon. What are you going to tell her?" Even as Connor gave the excuse, he felt bad, knowing full well it was he who needed Elizabeth to stay and be the glue that held this mess together.

Elizabeth shrugged her shoulders. "I don't know. Things are such a mess, Connor; I can't even explain why I need to know. I just do. But I won't go without your blessing." She looked at her husband once more, her gaze pleading with him to reconsider. Connor sighed, the deep sigh of a man who knows he's lost before the argument has even begun.

"You can't go alone," he said, his voice softening as he walked over and sat down next to his wife. "I can only take a couple of days off, but I'm going with you." Elizabeth flung her arms around him and kissed him. It wasn't the victory kiss of a woman who had gotten her way; rather, it was the kiss of genuine affection, genuine love, and genuine care. She pulled away from him and placed her hands on his face, looking into the eyes that enraptured her heart so many years ago.

"I'll never understand why I've been the lucky one," she said. "Ellen always wanted this, but it was always a step away and she was too impatient to wait. Do you think the things that elude us here are waiting for us in heaven?"

Connor placed his hands over his wife's and leaned in, kissing her once more. "I think God is merciful. At least, that's what my father always said. Whatever is waiting for us after we die is better than what we deserve."

As the plane landed on the tarmac in Cincinnati, the jitters that had been building in Elizabeth since take-off now felt like sumo wrestlers battling it out inside of her. The landscape looked grey and cold, almost foreboding. She reached over and instinctively grabbed Connor's hand, pulling from his strength.

The walk from the plane to the car rental kiosk didn't take long enough to settle her nerves. It was only going to be a quick overnight trip, but it felt like only seconds had passed since they left Chicago. They had come on blind faith, unable to reach the young woman by phone. They had no plan, no motives, and no idea what they were going to do beyond driving to the address provided by the investigator and hoping Christina was home.

By the time they got in the car, a light drizzle had descended on the city, fogging the windshield and affecting visibility on the road. The drive was spent in silence; the only sound coming from the computerized voice on the GPS telling them to turn left, right and eventually stop in front of a run-down apartment building.

The building sat in the Over-the-Rhine neighborhood and looked as tough on the outside as Connor was guessing the tenants were on the inside. Elizabeth stared at the building as thoughts of her first apartment flooded her mind. Eventually, Elizabeth chuckled as she thought of what they must look like, so obviously out of place. Their car, their faces, their clothes… everything about them said they didn't belong.

"We're adults," she said, looking at Connor, "grown ups, and we're scared stiff at the sight of this place."

"You're the one with the ghetto background," Connor said jokingly. "You're all uppity now, huh?"

"Come on," she said, opening her car door and stepping out into the cold air. Connor exited the car and quickly punched the lock button on his keypad, causing the beep to echo off the stone building. Several young boys hanging out in the doorway looked up at the noise, their conversation stopping. Elizabeth led Connor through the group and into the doorway, taking note of the missing door. The hinges were bent and the door had probably been long discarded. "Its apartment 3D," she said to Connor, leading him up the stairs as they walked past an elevator bearing a faded "Out of Order" sign.

When they arrived at the girl's apartment, Elizabeth knocked because there was no doorbell to push. The low hum of the TV came through the small crack at the bottom of the door. Elizabeth knocked again and this time they saw footsteps approach the door and someone look out of the peephole.

"Hello," Elizabeth said as brightly as she could muster. "My name is Elizabeth Templeton. I'm looking for Christina."

"Tina ain't here right now," a voice said on the other side. "She's at work."

"Oh. Do you know what time she'll be back?"

"What do you want?" the voice said, coughing a little.

"I want to talk to her about Jack Edwards," Elizabeth said, slowing down her speech as she said his name. There was a long pause, and then they heard the chain unlatch and the lock open from the other side. A woman in her mid to late 40's opened the door enough to get a look at them before opening it a little wider.

"What do you want to know about that bastard?" she said, sizing Elizabeth up and down with her eyes.

Elizabeth kept a steady gaze on the woman and took a chance. "Can we come in? I can assure you we're not friends of his." The woman looked at Elizabeth and then glanced at Connor before nodding and stepping aside.

She led them into what appeared to be a small one-bedroom apartment. There were toys scattered around the floor, and a young man was sitting a few inches from the television; his neck craned as he watched Sesame Street. He didn't move at all when they came in. The older woman walked over to him and gently touched his shoulder. She whispered something in his ear that made him get up and go back to the bedroom. When he passed Elizabeth, she couldn't help but gasp. It was as if she were looking down at a little Jack. Her heart sank.

"If you are looking for Jack, I don't know where he is. I haven't seen him in almost sixteen years," she said.

"We know where he is," Connor said awkwardly. The woman's eyes narrowed in suspicion.

"Are you here for Levi?" she said. "Is that what this is about? Jack wants Levi?" She stood up and made a step towards the bedroom, blocking them from the door.

"No, no," said Elizabeth. "This is all very uncomfortable, and I apologize for that. Maybe we should have called before we came. It's just..." she stopped and looked at Connor, who nodded, encouraging her just to get it out. "My sister married Jack over ten years ago. My sister had a little girl, Hannah, from another man, and recently my niece claimed Jack raped her. And now she's pregnant, so I hired an investigator, who found out about Christina and her son, so we decided to come and see you." Even Elizabeth

was surprised at how she was pouring out her family's secrets to a woman she barely knew. She sat still, barely breathing as she waited for the woman to respond.

The woman looked at Elizabeth in disbelief, her eyes piercing as if she were looking at the couple for the first time since they had arrived. "Jack got this girl pregnant?" she asked. "You sure?"

"She's not due for another three months, so we won't know for sure until the baby is born. Please, ma'am, can you please let me know about your daughter. I just…" she stopped and looked down at her folded hands gripping her purse. "I just have to know."

"My name is Ella," the woman said, sitting down on an old, tattered ottoman catty-corner from the couch. "Tina is my daughter, and Levi is my grandson." She paused as she looked over at the bedroom door to make sure it was closed. "And he's also Jack's son."

What came from her mouth next was washed in obscenities and aggression. She had met Jack at a local bar and took to him at once. He was sweet and kind, she had said, and was a natural ladies' man. Since she had gotten pregnant with Tina when she was only thirteen years old, most boys stayed away from her, seeing her as nothing more than a baby mama they could use for one-night stands. She thought Jack was different. He paid attention to her and showered her with affection. Even though he couldn't keep a job, she still let him move in. He seemed to genuinely be interested in Tina and would often volunteer to baby-sit while she worked late night shifts at the gas station. Tina was only five when they got together, and they stayed together for ten years.

"Did you ever marry?" asked Elizabeth, not recalling a wedding in the file.

"No, we never did. Jack never brought it up, and I never asked. It was different with me. I was only eighteen and I had a five-year-old. I never finished high school," she said, looking away from them as she spoke, "and my own mama kicked me out when I first started showing with Tina. Life with Jack wasn't perfect, but I thought it was the best I could get."

Ella went on to explain that around Tina's thirteenth birthday, things began to change. Tina started acting weird, and Jack started coming to Ella less and less for sexual pleasure. She kept asking him if there was another woman, and he would brush her aside, telling her she was crazy for even suggesting such a thing. It wasn't until Tina's fifteenth birthday Ella began to get suspicious. "I came home from work early one night and caught Jack coming out of her room. I asked him what was going on and he said Tina had had a bad dream. Like a stupid fool, I believed him. The day Tina turned fifteen was the day she found out she was pregnant. I found her crying in the bathroom and noticed the test in the sink. She was pregnant. She tried to kill herself." Ella's eyes filled with tears as she looked away. "It sent her off the deep end. She started getting into drugs and partying. It was months before she finally told me what Jack had done. I kicked that bastard out that same night."

Ella stopped as tears came down her face, highlighting the years of worry and hard living. "Maybe we shouldn't have come," Elizabeth said, feeling herself begin to lose control. "I'm so sorry we bothered you about all this. Come on, Connor," she said, motioning for him to follow her lead and exit the apartment.

"No," Ella interjected. "I'm glad you came. It was wrong what Jack did. He ruined my little girl's life, but the worst part," Ella stopped, and wiped away tears, "is Levi. He's not..." she stopped as she fumbled for the words. "He's not right in the head. All the drugs Tina did – it was unfair what happened to him."

Elizabeth's head was spinning as she looked around the apartment. The story was too sad, the apartment too grim, and the life this woman was laying out before her was too much to handle. Flashbacks of her mother, the funeral, her own life came through, making her feel dizzy. She felt Connor lead her back to the couch and heard Ella offer her a glass of cold water.

Ella watched her from the ottoman, waiting as Connor fretted over her. "Your sister," she finally said. "Is she still with Jack?"

Elizabeth nodded, "Yes, ma'am."

"Is your niece keeping the baby?"

"She hasn't decided."

"You know, that jerk hasn't given Levi anything," she said. "Not a penny. Even just a few dollars would be helpful." Connor looked at her and watched as her eyes flashed down towards Elizabeth's purse. He helped Elizabeth up and led her to the door.

"I'm sorry, but we should go," he said. "Thank you for your time. I wish things had been different for you, and for us." He opened the door and placed his coat over Elizabeth head to shield her from the rain as he followed her out of the apartment.

"Tell that bastard he owes my daughter money!" Ella yelled down the hallway.

Together, they walked down the steps; Connor gripping his wife's hand as they descended twice as fast as the trip up to the apartment. Once in the car, Connor locked all the doors and started the engine, pulling out of the parking lot before Elizabeth had even buckled her safety belt. He drove away from the apartment building until he felt a safe distance had passed. Pulling into a fast food parking lot, he turned to Elizabeth with a stern look on his face. "You have to tell your sister."

Elizabeth nodded. "Oh, my goodness, Connor," she said. "What kind of a man would do this?" Connor reached over and held his wife as she sobbed into his already wet rain jacket. He held his wife as they both sat in the car, travel weary and emotionally drained from the day's events. He thought of Hannah back at the house and of the baby growing inside her. Up until this point, he hadn't allowed himself to feel anything for the child, fearing Hannah would choose to give the baby away. He was intentional about remaining emotionless, but after seeing Ella and Levi crammed into a small apartment, a visible picture of the atrocities Jack was capable of, he couldn't help but reach out to the unborn child.

CHAPTER 24

Elizabeth's eyes were glued on Hannah. She could tell the young girl was trying to hold it together under the weight of what she had just been told. It had been almost a month since they had returned from Cincinnati. The weight of the news had lain heavy on them as they went back and forth about what to do with the information. Finally, it was Elizabeth who decided Hannah had a right to know.

Hannah sat awkwardly on the couch, the slump of a woman who was almost eight months pregnant. The once-juvenile face had changed throughout the past months as the broken relationship with her mother and the pregnancy took their toll on her body. Places she didn't even know could swell were sore and tired.

"I think I'm okay," she said slowly. Pulling her right leg up on the couch, she began to rub her ankle. "I mean, I guess it all makes sense. He just knows what kind of woman to look for."

"What do you mean?" Elizabeth asked, somewhat confused at the lack of emotion coming from Hannah.

"Desperate, Aunt Lizzie," she said. "He's the kind of man who picks out women in desperate situations and then screws their kid. I get it. Really, I do. He looks for women who are stupid enough to believe him." Elizabeth looked at Hannah, a worried expression visibly covering her face.

"Hannah, your mom's not stupid," she said, feeling the need to come to her sister's defense. "She fell in love with Jack. That doesn't make someone stupid."

"You know, the first time Jack touched me I almost vomited on him. Can you imagine?" Hannah laughed. "I guess if I had puked on his penis that *137* would have been the end of it." She pushed herself off the couch and looked at her aunt. "Now what?"

Elizabeth didn't stand up. She sat, looking up at her niece. "I think we should tell your mother." She watched as Hannah stood before her; her silhouette casting a shadow on the wall that highlighted her pregnant belly.

"Aunt Lizzie, I've tried to see things from my mom's point of view. I've tried to be in her shoes, to see what could happen in life that could make me choose a man over my own flesh and blood. I can't make it work. I can't think of a single thing my child could do that would make me turn my back on them and walk away," she snapped her fingers, "just like that. You can tell my mom, but I don't think she'll care."

"Hannah, please don't say that. Your grandmother would never have wanted… "

"My grandmother is dead," Hannah said abruptly. "No one even talks about her except you. Whatever or whoever she was it doesn't matter, Aunt Liz." She walked away, feeling lonely and afraid as she closed her bedroom door. She grunted and leaned against the chest of drawers as the baby kicked her hard. Her aunt wasn't the only one that had been hiding information from her. The day Connor and Elizabeth left for Ohio; Hannah had met with an adoption agency to officially sign the papers to give up her child. She had made the decision months ago, but couldn't face her aunt with the news. The papers had been signed. The deal was done. Within a matter of hours, the agency emailed over prospective couples. Hannah had quickly looked through the list and picked one at random. Anyone who took this baby home had to be in a better situation than her.

Hannah collected her pajamas and walked into the bathroom. She just needed to clear her head, to get all of the emotions swirling around inside of her out, to let the steam from the shower help her overcome. Sitting on the toilet for the twentieth time, she was surprised at how quick and how fast the urine came. "How can I still have any pee in me?" she muttered to herself. Only this time, something felt different. She couldn't stop the stream as it kept trickling out. She stood up, straddling the toilet when the pain hit her, shooting straight up her back. She let out a scream and fell against the sink counter. Breathing in and out, she tried to compose herself but before she could do anything, another round of pain shot up her back

This time the scream was louder as the intensity of the pain increased.

The bathroom door burst open and Connor was standing there looking down at her, half dressed and sitting on the floor. "Oh, God," he said quickly, "I'm so sorry. Are you – oh, my God, Hannah, are you in labor?" He reached down to help her up and she pushed him away.

"Get Lizzie!" she screamed as another pain shot up her back. It felt like someone was tightening a rubber band across her stomach, and pulling it as far as it would go. Just when she felt like she couldn't take the pain anymore, it would subside, leaving her out of breath and light-headed. She could hear Connor frantically screaming for his wife and then footsteps running down the hallway.

"Hannah?" Elizabeth stepped closer and her feet slipped on the puddle of water slowly forming under her. "Connor!" she yelled into the hallway. "Get the car, now! Hannah's having the baby!" Helping Hannah up, Elizabeth aided her in dressing. She grabbed a towel from the rack along with Hannah's overnight bag that had been packed for weeks. She laid Hannah down on the backseat and placed the towel underneath her backside. "Just try to take it easy," she said calmly as she jumped into the front seat beside Connor. "Go!" she yelled at him when he failed to move fast enough.

Connor floored it and peeled out of the driveway, hitting the garbage cans that were still at the curb from the morning's trash pickup. "Leave it!" Elizabeth yelled as Connor got out to get the cans.

"Right, sorry," said Connor, peeling out once again and down the road.

Oh, God, this can't be happening, thought Hannah as she sat in the backseat, doubled over from the pain. It's too soon. It's too early, was all she could think as the car raced through the city. Connor pulled the car directly up to the hospital emergency room entrance and helped Lizzie and Hannah out. They walked through the doors and into the emergency room. Within seconds of arriving, a nurse spotted them and hastily pushed over a wheelchair.

"How far along are you?" she asked Hannah.

"Only 36 weeks. It's too early," she breathed as another contraction wreaked havoc on her body altering her speech.

"Early or not, I'd say you were in labor," the woman said, pushing her into a side room. Another nurse came into the room and helped lift Hannah onto the bed. Elizabeth helped undress the girl and slipped a hospital gown over her body. "I'm just going to check your cervix," the nurse informed her. "She's at a ten," she said to Elizabeth. "Are you her mother?"

"No, no, I'm her aunt. What does all this mean?"

"It means she's having the baby and it's almost time to push." She radioed for a doctor, and within minutes, a young man who looked too young to be a doctor stepped into the room. He washed his hands in the sink and stepped over to Hannah. Reaching out, he held her hand with his and placed his other hand on her head.

"I'm Dr. Newbury," he said, "and it's going to be all right. You are about to have your baby. Just listen to the advice Lisa and I give you, and everything will be fine." He paused and smiled at her. "And don't be scared. People have babies every day."

"Yea, but I don't!" Hannah screamed as she prepared herself to push.

The labor was short but intense. Hannah went in and out, as contractions came and the nurses told her to push. Elizabeth didn't leave her niece's side, holding her hand and coaching her as best as she could through the entire thing. When the final push came and the baby came out, Hannah fell back on the bed, completely exhausted.

"Congratulations," one of the nurses said. "It's a beautiful baby boy." Hannah looked up through blurry eyes as the nurse held the baby in front of her.

"It's not my boy," Hannah mumbled. "It's not my baby." She turned her head and fainted, her mind going blank, as she finally was able to rest.

The hospital staff moved them to a smaller, more private recovery room. Hannah had lost a lot of blood and had torn badly. She was given pain medicine as they stitched her up. She still hadn't fully awakened.

Elizabeth was sitting beside her, staring into the face of a young woman she felt she hardly knew anymore. Even though they lived in the same house, her niece was not the same girl she was so many years ago. She was hardened; the pregnancy had built another wall around her already toughened fortress of a heart.

When Hannah fainted, the room became abuzz with activity. Elizabeth tried to stay calm; floating back and forth between the newborn and her niece, trying to piece together everything that had happened. When things quieted down, she called Dr. Monroe's office to let her know of the birth, and that's when she finally understood what Hannah had mumbled as she faded out of consciousness. Dr. Monroe told her of Hannah's decision to give up the baby. The only stipulation Hannah requested was that a DNA test be completed to determine for sure the father of the child. In the adoption papers, Hannah requested to not see the baby, to have it taken away as soon as it was born. The intensity of the labor had fulfilled her wishes, and in the aftermath of it all while she was still asleep, the hospital staff worked out the details with Dr. Monroe and the adoption agency.

Connor had gone down to the cafeteria to get a cup of coffee. He seemed to take the reality of the adoption harder than anyone. When he excused himself, there were tears in his eyes as he hurried out of the room and down the hall. Closing her eyes, Elizabeth's thoughts drifted to her mother. She hadn't thought of Mama in some time, but now more than ever she wished she could sit down before her and ask advice on what to do next. Things were so broken in their family that she couldn't imagine what could possibly fix them. It was like an old pair of jeans that had been mended one too many times. Eventually, the patches ran out and the jeans fell apart. She felt like everything was falling apart around her.

"Aunt Liz?" Elizabeth opened her eyes and looked at Hannah, who had finally come to.

"I'm right here, honey," she said and pulled her chair closer to the bed. "I'm right here."

Hannah looked around the room and back at her aunt. "How long have I been out?"

"Just a few hours... They gave you some pretty strong pain meds. You tore pretty badly." Hannah moved her arm and winced as the needle from the IV pinched her skin. She looked off into the distance, the emptiness in her eyes revealing the despondency in her heart. She was thinking to herself, *Lord, why me?* Hating herself more for allowing this to happen to her. Not *141* really caring, but feeling she should ask... "Is the baby…" her words trailed off; she was not able to bring herself to finish the sentence.

"The hospital staff took him away, just as you requested," said Elizabeth with disappointment in her tone. She had been hoping Hannah would allow her to keep the baby, but she stopped herself from saying more. At these words, Hannah looked away, realizing her aunt knew. "Hannah," Elizabeth said softly, "why didn't you tell us you wanted to give the baby away? We could have helped you think through it."

Tears were coming from Hannah's eyes, but she didn't bother to wipe them away. "I knew you would try to talk me out of it. I'm so sorry," she said, finally losing it. Elizabeth grabbed her niece and held her body as it once again heaved with the sobs emerging from deep within. "I'm so sorry," she said once more, feeling like a limp rag in her aunt's arms.

"Oh, Hannah," Elizabeth said, trying to keep her composure. "It doesn't matter. You did what you thought was best, and that's all that matters." Elizabeth's voice was choking as she held her niece in disappointment.

After a few moments had passed, Hannah finally pulled back from her aunt. "Does my mom know?" she asked weakly.

Elizabeth shook her head. "No, I haven't told her. I wanted to wait until you could tell me what you wanted me to do." Elizabeth looked down at her niece and saw that, once again, her eyes were fluttering, the pain medicine making it difficult for her to stay awake for too long. "You know what?" she said as she stroked her hair. "Let's just think about this later. Why don't you go back to sleep?" Hannah's eyes were already closed, and Elizabeth could see her rhythmic breathing.

She stepped out of the room, longing for some fresh air trying to put some distance between herself and what just happened. She couldn't help but notice the scene in the room across the hall as grandparents rushed past her, carrying balloons and wrapped packages. There was a collective cheer from the group inside as a small, swaddled baby was presented and placed in the grandmother's arms. One of the guests walked over and closed the door, blocking Elizabeth from the celebration. She leaned her head against the wall and rubbed her temples. The emotions of the day had left her with a pounding headache.

"Coffee?" asked Connor, gently touching her elbow and lifting a to-go cup in front of her. "I made it just the way you like it." She smiled at him and reached for the cup, but her hand knocked it out of his, the lid popping off as it hit the floor spilling coffee all over the linoleum.

"Oh, my goodness, I'm so sorry," she said, stooping to mop up the mess with whatever she could find. Hunched over the floor, looking at the spilled coffee, she lost it. She sat in the middle of the floor, sobbing, holding onto Connor as he bent down to help. He sat down beside his wife, feeling the coffee seep through his pants but not caring. The chaos of the moment seemed to fit the situation. Her sobs echoed off the floor, causing a few people to look outside their doors. One of the nurses came over and helped Connor lift Elizabeth, offering to clean up the mess. She gently led them into an unoccupied room, telling them to take as much time as they needed.

"Lizzie," said Connor gently, "it's going to be all right. Hannah is healthy, the baby is placed with a good family… it's going to be okay." Elizabeth wanted to believe he was right. She wanted to be optimistic, but in the moment she felt so beat-down and threadbare. The crying was making her headache even more intense. She rubbed her temples once more, wanting to believe Connor's optimism, and then everything went black.

"Mama, do you believe in God?" Elizabeth asked. She watched as Rose looked up from her sewing machine, studying the face of her young daughter.

"Of course," she said. "Don't you?"

Elizabeth shrugged. "I don't know. If there's a God, why do you feel so sad sometimes? I heard you crying last night," she confessed.

The sewing machine rested on an old end table at the foot of Rose's bed. She took off her glasses and walked over to her daughter, joining her on the bed. The mattress sunk under the additional weight. "Baby, I cry because sometimes I don't know what to do. I cry because I'm not sure what to do with life. I cry because I believe in God, but I can't always see His face."

"I thought God was invisible, Mama." Elizabeth was fiddling with a thread from the mattress, slowly pulling out the seam.

"God's not invisible. He just looks different than you think, different then I think. Sometimes you see Him best when you're not looking for Him, I guess."

"Do you see God?" The innocence of the question took Rose by surprise.

"I see Him in you."

℧

When Elizabeth came to, she was lying on the bed in the room, but this time it was Connor who was playing the nursemaid. "You blacked out," he said, his forehead wrinkled with worry. She stood up slowly, taking her time as the room came into focus.

"I'm okay," she said. "We should get back to Hannah." She walked past him before he could object.

CHAPTER 25

"Are you nervous?" Connor asked her. Hannah looked at her uncle as if he had asked her if the grass was green. "Okay," he acknowledged, "stupid question." She sat beside him at the kitchen table, clutching the paperwork in her hands. Inside was the test that would change everything for her. If it showed her stepfather to be the father of the baby, she could then live in peace with her decision to let the boy go. If it proved otherwise, she didn't know how she could live with herself.

Her hands shook as she fiddled with the envelope. Her aunt was nervously watching from across the table, sipping coffee in a comforting, familiar manner. Hannah had promised her if Jack was the father of the baby, they would finally confront her mother about his past. She had been able to put this off for almost two months while they waited for the test results, but now it was the final hour;, the moment when everything in her life would change once again, for good or bad. She pulled the piece of paper out and read the results, quickly scanning the jargon to get to what really mattered.

"Well?" her aunt said, the tension in the room thick enough to feel.

Hannah looked up at her aunt and uncle, the ones who had taken her in when she had nowhere else to go. She hated putting them through this and she hated the grey hairs and wrinkles she had brought upon them since she moved in.

'Before I tell you," she said, "I just want you both to know how grateful I am for everything you've done. I, um," Hannah stopped, her voice choking over the words. "I don't know what would have happened if you weren't willing to take me." She paused, but her aunt and uncle said nothing. When she finally opened her mouth once more, the words rolled out slowly. "Jack was the father." *145*

Without saying anything, Connor got up from the table, picked up his keys and got in the car. Elizabeth sat staring at the door to the garage; her mouth slightly agape, surprised by his reaction. "I guess it's time to go," she said, looking at Hannah and smiling. "Better late than never, right?"

Hannah nodded. After all of these months, what she wanted more than anything was to begin putting her life back together. She knew this final confrontation was the first step in the process of moving forward, with or without her mother beside her. At least she had the proof of science in her corner this time.

When they arrived at the apartment and Ellen answered the door, the look of shock was written all over her face. "What…" she started, "what are you doing here?" Elizabeth pushed past her sister and walked into the apartment, Hannah and Connor following her.

"I'm doing something I should have done a long time ago, Ellen. Is Jack here?" Ellen shook her head, surprised at the level of determination in her baby sister. "The kids? Where are they?"

"At a friend's house," she replied. "She's watching them for the day so I can get some rest," she said. Gaining her composure, she added, "But that's none of your business. I don't remember inviting you in."

Elizabeth held up a hand to stop her sister. "I've stood silently by long enough, Ellen. I grew up with you, remember? I sat in my bed at night listening as you climbed in the window of your bedroom, sneaking off with too many boys to count. I don't know what happened to you that made you always want to be with a man, but now it's gone too far. I've let you down, I've let Hannah down, and I've let Mama down by sitting silently like a coward through this entire thing. I've watched you forsake your daughter and throw yourself at a man that can't even provide for you and your family. It all ends today, Ellen," she said and grabbed the paperwork from Hannah's hands, thrusting it into Ellen's. "Go on," she said to her niece. "Tell your mother."

The strength pouring from Elizabeth had overflowed into Hannah, who found herself standing visibly straighter as she looked at her mother. "The baby was Jack's, Mama. And I have the test results to prove it." Tears were forming in her eyes, but this time she wasn't the one shaking. She watched

Ellen's trembling hand as the weight of what she held in her hands washed over her.

"I don't understand," she said, looking back at her sister and daughter. "I mean, he said he didn't do it. He said you lied about everything."

"He did do it, mama, and he's done it before."

"What do you mean 'before?'?" Ellen asked, but before she could get an answer, they all turned towards the door as Jack entered. He stopped short in the doorway as soon as he saw the mob gathered in the front room. His expression of rage turned to fear when he saw the look on Ellen's face.

"Ellen?" he said cautiously. "What's going on?" Staring down at the paper, Ellen couldn't even bring herself to speak. She looked at her sister Elizabeth, pleading with her eyes for her to intervene.

"What's going on, Jack," Elizabeth began, "is that it's over. The lies, the deceit — it's all over."

Jack walked over to Ellen and grabbed her by the shoulders, "Don't listen to them, Ellen," he pleaded. "I swear on our love, on our kids, I did not touch her." Ellen shook his hands off of her. He screamed, "I love you!"

"Love? Love? Don't tell me about love! You don't know the first thing about love, because love don't hurt, love will not have sex with their wife's daughter. You don't know the first thing about love!" Ellen screamed. " Get off of me," she said through clenched teeth. "How dare you stand here and lie to me again, you bastard. I believed you! You looked right in my face and lied to me!"

Ellen pushed him away, hard this time, surprising herself at her own strength. He tripped over the coffee table and landed on the couch. He looked from Ellen to Elizabeth and, jumping up, lunged at Elizabeth. Connor was quick to jump in front of his wife, causing Jack to stop short. "Don't you even think hitting her," Connor said adamantly.

"It's over, Jack," Ellen said again.

"Maybe we should call Christina and ask her what to believe," Elizabeth said. There was fire in his eyes at the mention of her name.

"What did that girl tell you?" he demanded of Elizabeth. "That I raped her? She's just looking for someone to pin her idiot kid on. Don't let her do this, Ellen," he said, moving towards his wife once again. "She's filling your head *147* with all of these lies."

"What lies, Jack? Listen to yourself. You sound pathetic. It's over, Jack!" Elizabeth shouted, her voice rising in frustration.

"Over?" Jack hissed. "It will never be over between us." With fire in his eyes, he lunged for Elizabeth. This time he was prepared, his eyes wild with fury. Connor lunged at Jack once again, but Jack hit him with a strong uppercut, sending him flying backwards. Hannah ran toward her aunt, but it was too late. Jack punched her hard in the face, causing her to fall back, knocked out from the blow. Screaming, Hannah fumbled in her purse for her phone, but before she could make the call, she ran to help her mother. Jack had her by the throat, pushing her up against the wall.

Ellen stared at her husband, gasping for breath and trying to scratch at him with her nails. Hannah was clawing at her stepfather, trying hard to get him to release his grip on Ellen. She was beginning to see stars, and the room was spinning in a hazy fog.

☙

Ellen leaned against the veranda on the old house, gaining her balance as her head spun dizzily from the beers at the party. The autumn air was crisp and cool against her flesh. She was wearing a halter top and tight jeans. They were inappropriate for the weather but they made her feel like a million bucks at a party. Although Ellen was beautiful for her age, it was obvious to anyone at the party she was too young to be there. She was only in the eighth grade, yet received the invitation to a senior party from an older friend at school. She spent hours searching in her wardrobe for the perfect outfit, waited until everyone was asleep at home, and then slipped out of the window to sneak to the party. The exhilaration kept her going until the beers eventually caught up with her.

"You okay?" She turned her head and saw Randy walking out of the house. He had been following her around the house all night, trying to get her to dance with him, drink with him, anything. Up until now, she had been polite with his advances, but this guy just wasn't taking the hint.

"I'm fine, Randy," she said, the tone of her voice bearing the annoyance she felt inside. "Just go back into the party. I'm fine." He walked up to her and kissed her on the shoulder. "What the hell?" she said, spinning around t face him. "What do you think you're doing?"

"Come on, Ellen," he said, "quit fighting it. You know I like you. Let's just make this easy."

She pushed him away and started towards the door. "I just want to go home," she said. He grabbed her wrist from behind and pulled her in, forcing a kiss. She pushed him away again and made a run for the door.

Randy grabbed her waist from behind and lifted her feet off the porch. She was no match for the football player. He jumped over the low porch wall, bringing her with him. As much as she was kicking and fighting, she felt like a limp rag doll in his massive hands. He pushed her to the ground on the side of the house, and she winced at the pain of sticks and rocks that pushed against her flesh. "Don't scream, baby," he taunted her, holding her hands over her head and unzipping his jeans. "Play nice and I won't even tell anybody what a slut you are."

"Randy, please," she begged, "you don't need to do this. I'll go out on a date with you, I promise. Just get off me." He ignored her pleas and pressed a handkerchief in her mouth. Her body shuddered from the cold and the weight of his body as he pressed into her.

It didn't last long. He did his business and, when he was done, leaned down, and whispered in her ear, "If you tell anyone about this, I have friends who would love to screw a whore." He licked her face, adding humiliation to the list of atrocities.

She lay on the ground and watched him as he walked away. Her stomach lurched from the alcohol and the encounter, causing her to vomit on the frozen ground, some of it splashing up on her jeans. Dressing once again, she walked away from the house to the nearest bus stop. Slipping through her bedroom window, she curled up on her bed and cried herself to sleep.

Hannah's lunges at her stepfather eventually caused him to loosen his grip on her mother. With the temporary release from her neck, Ellen gasped for air. As soon as Ellen felt the mercy, she struggled away from her husband and ran into the bedroom, closing and locking the door behind her. She could hear Hannah screaming from the living room as she opened the nightstand and pulled out the small handgun Jack kept hidden in the back. 149

Her hands were shaking as she loaded and cocked the gun, trembling when she realized she could no longer hear Hannah.

Ellen strained, listening for any sign of movement in the apartment. Fearing the worst, she began to move towards the bedroom door, when suddenly the door burst inward, kicked in by Jack, knocking a picture off the wall. Screaming, she closed her eyes, pulled the trigger, and let off three shots, the gunshots ringing through the thin walls of the apartment. Jack fell face down on top of Ellen. She could hear screams from downstairs as everyone thought Jack shot her.

She dropped the gun and pushed Jack's limp body off her as the blood began to leak from his chest. She ran into the living room in panic and leaned down over Hannah. A bruise was forming over her daughter's eye as she lay on the ground, tears streaming down her face.

"Baby, are you alright?" Ellen said. Connor was bent over Liz, tending to her as she started to come to from the blackout.

The police car lights lit up the apartment.

CHAPTER 26

Elizabeth and Connor each lifted a sleeping child from the car, carrying Ivy and Tyson in their arms. They walked them to their own bedroom and, making palettes for them on the floor, returned to the kitchen. Elizabeth made coffee and waited.

The night had been a blur of activity once the police arrived and found the scene at the apartment. The paramedics rushed Jack to the hospital while statements were given, evidence collected, and Ellen taken in for questioning. Hannah had driven to the police station to wait it out and bring Ellen to their home when everything was done.

They didn't know what to say so they sat at the kitchen table in silence and waited. When the car finally pulled into the driveway, neither of them got up from the table it was all too surreal; the evening had seemed like a dream.

Hannah entered the room first, her mascara still smudged on her face, looking absolutely exhausted. Ellen followed the look of shock still on her face. "I'm fine," she said, before anyone could ask. "They haven't charged me with anything. They said it's a pretty clear case of self-defense." The coffee machine beeped to let them know brewing was finished. It sounded hollow in the silence of the kitchen.

"Are you hungry?" Elizabeth asked, not able to think of anything else to say, of anything else she had to offer her sister.

"No. I just want to talk to Hannah alone, if that's all right."

"Of course," said Connor, getting up from the table. "The kids are in our bedroom. You can sleep there or with Hannah. We'll be in the guest room on the second floor." He hugged Hannah awkwardly as he passed and *151* grabbed his wife's hand as they wearily walked up the stairs.

Hannah poured herself a cup of coffee and sat down at the table. Ellen followed. "I'm sorry, baby," she said, looking down at the ground. "I let you down, and I'll never forgive myself for not doing anything." She didn't expect Hannah to say anything, and when her daughter returned the apology with silence, she continued. "I should have been able to see the signs. I ignored so many things. I was supposed to protect you. As your mother, I was supposed to protect you. Please forgive me."

Hannah's fingers traced the rim of her coffee cup as she sat thinking about the night's events. "I think we're past forgiveness, Mama," she said. Her voice wasn't angry, but it wasn't affectionate either. She thought of the long months of pregnancy, the pain of delivery and the heartache of watching her child be taken away, and she wondered how she could ever feel close to her mother again.

"I know it's no excuse," said Ellen, "but I was raped, about the same age as when Jack…" she stopped, unable to say the taboo words. Hannah's head turned towards her mother's; her facial expression softening. "I had been invited to a high school party — a senior party, you know. I thought I was big stuff. And there was a boy there from the neighborhood who had been eyeing me like a hawk for weeks. He followed me around like a lion hunting prey. As soon as he saw me in a vulnerable position, he attacked. He forced himself on me and said if I told anyone he would send his friends to do the same. I was crushed. And I was never the same again." Ellen wiped the tears from her cheeks. "I've never told anyone that before, baby. But I think you should know."

"What did you do?" Hannah asked, timidly opening up a small part of her soul to her mother.

"I decided I was going to be the one who used instead of the one who got used," she looked at her daughter. "I've lived a pretty pitiable life. I wanted so much more for you, and I saw Jack and did the same thing all over again. Things were going to be different," she said, her voice breaking up despite her best efforts at keeping things under control. "I was going to give you more."

Hannah sighed deeply and looked over at her mother. "I don't know why things turned out the way they did. When you left me, Mama, I was lonely at such a deep level. I was pregnant without you. I had a baby without you. I gave my baby up without you." She turned away from her mother. "But I don't want to keep living moments without you. I need you, Mama," she said, her façade of strength coming down.

"I wanted things to be so different," Ellen said, embracing her daughter as they both cried deep tears of sorrow and relief. "I'm so sorry." They stayed in each other's arms, neither one in a hurry to pull back. Finally, it was Hannah who broke the silence.

"What happened to my daddy?" Hannah finally asked. For the first time in her life, she felt brave enough to broach the subject with her mother.

The question took Ellen by surprise, and she stared at her daughter. "Your father?" she asked. "We were in love," she said, and then added, "for a little bit. Things were hot and heavy, and then they were done. I was in school, and when I found out I was having you, you became my motivation to keep going. I wanted you to have all the things I grew up wanting."

"What was he like?" Hannah prodded again.

Ellen sighed. "He was smart and funny, an engineering major who was two years ahead of me. I thought he was an answered prayer." She stroked her daughter's hair.

"Did he know about me?"

"Yes, I told him about you," Ellen said slowly, "and let's just say he didn't take it that well. He yelled at me for being careless, and then transferred schools. That was that." She stared down at her daughter, searching for the perfect words. When they didn't come, she said, "Hannah, I kept you because you came from a place of love. You aren't bad for giving away your baby. Maybe in giving him away, you saved him."

"Why did this happen to us?" Hannah whispered. "I ask that question about twenty times a day, but I never get an answer."

"I don't know why," Ellen said. "I know it's not your fault. I know you didn't do anything to deserve it. Sometimes bad things happen to good people. The only thing you can control is what you do moving forward. Make your life better than mine. Don't let this hold you back."

Hannah dumped the remains of her coffee in the sink and turned towards her bedroom. "You coming?" she asked her mom.

"No, I think I should go upstairs with Ivy and Tyson. I want to be there when they wake up in the morning." Hannah nodded and walked back to her bedroom, leaving Ellen standing alone in the kitchen. Turning the kitchen lights off, she left the darkness of the room and headed toward the light of the stairs.

www.ingramcontent.com/pod-product-compliance
Lightning Source LLC
Chambersburg PA
CBHW071344170626
46811CB00003B/980